SILVER RESCUE

SEAL Brotherhood: Silver Team
Book 3

SHARON HAMILTON

SHARON HAMILTON'S BOOK LIST

SEAL BROTHERHOOD BOOKS

SEAL BROTHERHOOD SERIES
Accidental SEAL Book 1

Fallen SEAL Legacy Book 2

SEAL Under Covers Book 3

SEAL The Deal Book 4

Cruisin' For A SEAL Book 5

SEAL My Destiny Book 6

SEAL of My Heart Book 7

Fredo's Dream Book 8

SEAL My Love Book 9

SEAL Encounter Prequel to Book 1

SEAL Endeavor Prequel to Book 2

Ultimate SEAL Collection Vol. 1 Books 1-4 /
2 Prequels

Ultimate SEAL Collection Vol. 2 Books 5-9

SEAL BROTHERHOOD LEGACY SERIES
Watery Grave Book 1

Honor The Fallen Book 2

Grave Injustice Book 3

Deal With The Devil Book 4

Cruisin' For Love Book 5

Destiny of Love Book 6

Heart of Gold Book 7

Father's Dream Book 8

Second Time Love Book 9

Little Miracles Novella

SEAL BROTHERHOOD SILVER TEAM SERIES

Something About Silver Book 1

Loving Harper Book 2

Silver Rescue Book 3

BAD BOYS OF SEAL TEAM 3 SERIES

SEAL's Promise Book 1

SEAL My Home Book 2

SEAL's Code Book 3

Big Bad Boys Bundle Books 1-3

BAND OF BACHELORS SERIES

Lucas Book 1

Alex Book 2

Jake Book 3

Jake 2 Book 4

Big Band of Bachelors Bundle

BONE FROG BROTHERHOOD SERIES

New Year's SEAL Dream Book 1

SEALed At The Altar Book 2

SEALed Forever Book 3

SEAL's Rescue Book 4

SEALed Protection Book 5

Bone Frog Brotherhood Superbundle

BONE FROG BACHELOR SERIES
Bone Frog Bachelor Book 0.5

Unleashed Book 1

Restored Book 2

Revenge Book 3

Legacy Book 4

SUNSET SEALS SERIES
SEALed at Sunset Book 1

Second Chance SEAL Book 2

Treasure Island SEAL Book 3

Escape to Sunset Book 4

The House at Sunset Beach Book 5

Second Chance Reunion Book 6

Love's Treasure Book 7

Finding Home Book 8

Sunset SEALs Duet #1

Sunset SEALs Duet #2

LOVE VIXEN
Bone Frog Love

SHADOW SEALS
Shadow of the Heart

Shadow Warrior

SILVER SEALS SERIES

SEAL Love's Legacy

SLEEPER SEALS SERIES
Bachelor SEAL

STAND ALONE BOOKS & SERIES
SEAL's Goal: The Beautiful Game
Nashville SEAL: Jameson
True Blue SEALS: Zak
Paradise: In Search of Love
Love Me Tender, Love You Hard

NOVELLAS
SEAL You In My Dreams Magnolias and Moonshine

PARANORMALS

FREE TO LOVE SERIES
Free As A Bird Book 1
Romance Book 2
Science Of The Heart Book 3
The Promise Directive Book 4
New Beginnings Book 5

GOLDEN VAMPIRES OF TUSCANY SERIES
Honeymoon Bite Book 1
Mortal Bite Book 2
Christmas Bite Book 3
Midnight Bite Book 4

THE GUARDIANS
Heavenly Lover Book 1
Underworld Lover Book 2
Underworld Queen Book 3
Redemption Book 4

FALL FROM GRACE SERIES
Gideon: Heavenly Fall

SUNSET BEACH SERIES
I'll Always Love You
Back To You

NOVELLAS
SEAL Of Time: Trident Legacy

All of Sharon's books are available on Audible,
narrated by the talented J.D. Hart.

ABOUT THE BOOK

Former SEAL Hamish McDougal and the rest of Silver Team are tasked with uprooting and eliminating an immigrant smuggling operation that trafficks young teens at the southern border. They are aware of this group's international ties to larger groups outside the US, but they soon discover an unlikely US connection which makes their mission even more dangerous.

The Silver Team members are experienced operators from several branches of service and government, but this task will pit them against some of the most evil cartel allies, even more deadly than those they encountered while serving overseas.

The mission takes on a more personal risk when one of the members' family herself becomes a victim.

AUTHOR'S NOTE

I always dedicate my SEAL Brotherhood books to the brave men and women who defend our shores and keep us safe. Without their sacrifice and that of their families—because a warrior's fight always includes his or her family—I wouldn't have the freedom and opportunity to make a living writing these stories. They sometimes pay the ultimate price so we can debate, argue, go have coffee with friends, raise our children, and see them have children of their own.

One of my favorite tributes to warriors resides on many memorials, including one I saw honoring the fallen of WWII on an island in the Pacific:

> "When you go home
> Tell them of us, and say,
> For your tomorrow,
> We gave our today."

These are my stories created out of my own imagination. Anything that is inaccurately portrayed is either my mistake or done intentionally to disguise something I might have overheard over a beer or in the corner of one of the hangouts along the Coronado Strand.

I support two main charities. Navy SEAL/UDT Museum operates in Ft. Pierce, Florida. Please learn about this wonderful museum, all run by active and former SEALs and their friends and families, and who rely on public support, not that of the United States Government.

www.navysealmuseum.org

I also support Wounded Warriors, who tirelessly bring together the warrior as well as the family members who are just learning to deal with their soldier's condition and have nowhere to turn. It is a long path to becoming well, but I've seen first-hand what this organization does for its warriors and the families who love them. Please give what your heart tells you is right. If you cannot give, volunteer at one of the many service centers all over the United States. Get involved. Do something meaningful for someone who gave so much of themselves, to families who have paid the price for your freedom. You'll find a family there unlike any other on the planet.

www.woundedwarriorproject.org

CHAPTER 1

HAMISH MCDOUGALL, TEAM member of the elite Silver Team group and former Navy SEAL explosives expert on SEAL Team 5, was sitting in his oversized hot tub with all twenty jets going.

It was the perfect time of day, he thought. The moments after all the activity was done and just before the mysteries of the dark night ahead. Whether away in foreign lands or here at home, as he was now, it didn't matter. Night always had all the unexpected things. Some were dangerous, some were thrilling in a good way, but night was always unpredictable.

Coronado was crowned in a deep orange glow, like they'd been transported to Valhalla, just like the ancients had foretold. Huge puffy clouds danced in the darkening sky, picking up those golden outlines and purple hues, despite there barely being a breeze. The garden beyond still smelled ripe and fresh, not damp.

He was sipping a Scotch whisky.

The early fall weather in San Diego was also his favorite, as he leaned back and luxuriated in the foamy water. It was part rehabilitation and part spiritual experience for him. It was one daily requirement he didn't object to, ever since his knee surgery barely six months ago. It was his second full replacement. First one was done by a young Navy doctor fresh out of medical school to repair an old rugby injury that never healed right.

Now he was nearly fully rehabilitated. The warm soak in the hot tub was exactly what he liked to do at the end of every day, sipping whisky and getting prepared for hopefully a good night's rest.

It wasn't always easy for him to sleep. There were so many battles and deployments, so many things he'd seen that he couldn't unsee. Sleep was more precious to him than money these days. It was second to sex, but a close second.

He was getting ready to work up so that he could deploy again with the Silver Team on their next mission. He'd missed their last one due to his surgery.

Sasha, his fourteen-year-old daughter, and several of her friends as well as his two sons and oldest daughter came running out into the yard like a jabbering flock of turkeys. They danced around the hot tub, singing a silly song they'd picked up from the internet, making fun of each other. Their chattering reminded him of a string of blackbirds that liked to balance on the telephone wires at the back of his property.

The stillness of the moment was completely shattered. But he looked at the vibrant life of these youngsters, half of them being raised under his roof and the other half by friends or other former teammates. He was happy for their exuberance, for their zest for life. He celebrated their energy and felt blessed. He was stressed, of course, and he couldn't think straight, but he was blessed.

"D-a-d," Sasha said as she soldered up to the side and smiled at him. She poked her head over the edge of the tub to check to make sure he was wearing trunks. "Oh, good."

This was going to be an ask. He knew this. He had to explain himself. "I never know when you guys are going to come running in. Besides, your mother's not here, so no reason to be naked anyway."

She tossed her head back and giggled, as did several of the other kids.

"T.M.I., Dad," said Ian, his youngest son, his voice cracking, slurping the words through his new red, white, and blue braces.

Every time he looked at Ian, it was painful for Hamish. He had such a long way to go to become the strong man he knew the boy would be some day, beginning to get peach fuzz on his upper lip and

wearing silly surfer clothes, experiencing the embarrassment of dandruff, bad breath, and body odor all at
the same time. Hamish wouldn't trade places with him
for anything, just so he wouldn't have to go through
what poor Ian was going through now.

He remembered what his gran had told him. "All
those tough things you have to face as a helpless child
make you into the man you become."

But it was so awful to watch. Angie had a much
better attitude about it.

Sasha continued to stretch out her words, being coy
and careful. "Well, we were wondering if we could go
down and get some ice cream. And we'll bring you
back your favorite, of course! Or a whole quart if you
like. Can we borrow the car?"

"How many of you are there?" he asked while looking at the crowd. "Anymore inside I'm not seeing?"

"There's seven of us. No, everyone's outside. But
afterwards, if it's okay with you, we'd like to go for a
swim."

"Of course you would. That's just what I was thinking of doing. Think I'll sit here a little while longer in
peace while you guys go down to the ice cream shop."

"So I can get the keys from Mom and tell her you
said it was okay?"

"Yes, dear. And you can bring me back some Rocky
Road, of course."

"Oh, you're the best!" she said leaning over to give him a kiss on his sweaty forehead.

Sasha was such a beauty, just like her older sister, looking more and more like her mother every day. Hamish was thinking about all of the predictions his Scottish grandmother had made for him. She followed runes—pieces of bird bones, shells, and rocks she kept tucked into a tiny box by her bed. She consulted it every morning and every night before she said her prayers. Her old Highland ways would never be usurped by any Bible teaching.

She used to tell him they were descended from a clan of giants that used to roam all over the Scottish Highlands centuries ago. She claimed they could move huge boulders and build roads and bridges still standing centuries later. They may have even been responsible for helping to build monuments and rock formations in England. She claimed the tribe came over with the Vikings to conquer Scotland many years ago.

Hamish was over six foot six—four inches taller than Harper Cunningham, his boss on the Silver Team. And Hamish easily outweighed him by fifty pounds as well.

Growing up in California, his parents entered him in caber tosses and different Highland games for festivals that would come to town in California, and he was usually the top caber tosser or deadweight lifter. He also could dance, but that wasn't something he admitted or did in mixed company.

How his grandmother would look at him today! Domesticated and still in an active trade. Although not a Navy SEAL, he still did the work the SEALs sometimes started. Working for a semisecret organization, still doing good, still protecting the innocent. His grandmother would be so proud.

He could almost hear her speak to him. She'd told him not to pay too much attention to the girls until he was much, much older, since even at ten or twelve years old, he was often mistaken for being an adult. By fourteen, he could pass as old enough to drink.

True to his roots, he enjoyed a good sipping whisky. He never drank cheap whisky, although he did try some experimental blends, which he didn't much care for. He was an old-fashioned hero, the kind of guy who liked wines with simple names, either white or red table wines. He liked cars that drove fast and didn't take a lot of upkeep, and he liked his family: His loving wife of thirty-plus years, Angie, and his four beautiful children. It was a life that filled his heart with gladness and pride.

Angie had her bathing suit on and came out the back door to join him.

"Care for some company, Hamish?"

"Always, love of my life. Did you happen to bring the bottle?"

"Hamish, I know you're not on the pills any longer, but you're not supposed to drink too much either."

She didn't get in the tub, waiting for his response.

"This is my first, sweetheart. Allow me a second and I promise to kiss you all over your body tonight."

Her laugh was still angelic. "Well, you could've told me it was your second or third, and I still would've done it. Hang on. I'll be right back."

She returned with the bottle and had a fistful of ice in the other hand, which she dumped in his glass. She poured him enough to almost fill the top.

"That enough?"

"It's perfect, my love. Now get yourself in here so I can start the kissing."

Angie chuckled again. Even at fifty years of age, she was still strikingly beautiful, his one and only, the only woman in the whole world he ever loved. He would die without her by his side.

This was partly the reason he had such a strong bond with Harper, who felt the same for Lydia.

"I should warn you," he said as he lovingly watched her slip into the tub across from him, "the kids are coming back soon with their ice cream. It's only going to be nice out here for a few minutes."

"Noted. I figured. And I'm supposed to tell you that

Harper may stop by this evening, if you're available. He called a few minutes ago. He's in town."

"Oh? What did he want?" asked Hamish.

Angie clinked glasses with him and then took a sip. "Probably about the next mission. He asked me how you were doing. I told him I thought you were pretty much good to go. I hope I didn't say something I wasn't supposed to."

"Now, that's not quite classified. You did good, Angie. Come here. I need to kiss you now."

Angie slid over next to him on the bench, leaned in, and they shared a long sensuous kiss. When they broke apart, Angie fanned herself then splashed water in his face.

"I will say one thing, Hamish McDougall. I think your kisses have gotten better with age. I really do."

"Exactly what I was thinking—about you!"

HARPER ARRIVED ABOUT an hour later, just as Hamish was considering going in the pool. Angie had gone inside to take a shower and get ready for an early evening. The kids had still not come home yet. Angie was going to give Cora a call.

"You bring your trunks?"

"Nah. Didn't pack them. And no, I'm not going in the buff."

It was good to see Harper. It had been over a

month since they'd last had face-to-face communication.

"You're looking fit. Are you all shriveled up yet?" Harper asked.

"Just about. On what Angie requires of me this evening, I may not be able to perform. I may not be even able to find myself," he said, looking down between his legs.

They both laughed.

"Glad to see you still have your sense of humor. No issues with the knee?"

"Just stiff occasionally. Right as rain."

"Well, as you might guess, I wanted to see how you were doing. I know we've talked on the phone, but I thought I'd see it with my own eyes. We're probably due for something coming up—at least I was told this would be about the time. I just needed to know if you were going to be able to be on the team. You know, getting a second knee replacement is a big deal."

"Well, the first time around, the Navy did it, and I think they used all the new docs on me, even dental students maybe, if you know what I mean. That old rugby injury just never healed right. Then I thought they fixed it with surgery, but it still never was right and kept getting worse. So now with the Silver Team and our great insurance package and the extra funds, I got the number one knee guy in all of San Diego. I got a winner, Harper. I'm already out of pain, and I was barely two weeks after surgery. The hardware and the technology they have now compared to twenty years ago, well, it's like night and day. Everything was easier."

"Good to hear it. That's what Angie has told me too. So you're able to get a full medical clearance if we get something coming up? I don't want you to bail on me at the last minute. I need to know who I can count on."

"You can count on me. No question about it."

They chatted about various things having to do with their families. Lydia was enjoying being a mother, and they were considering going for number two.

"I knew that would happen. I've got built-in babysitters, if you guys will move down here to Coronado," said Hamish.

"Not on your life. She loves Sonoma County, and that's where we're gonna stay. Besides, with the property and everything that went on, she feels pretty safe there. And that's a big thing. We're harder to get to there. You guys—it's a little bit different."

"In all fairness, I don't have the target on my back like you did."

"Still do, I'm reminded. We're careful. But even for you and the family here, you know you gotta be vigilant. Be careful with those kids."

"You're saying my kids are going to get into trouble?" Hamish asked, a little bit worried.

"Not them. It's the people who hang around kids like that. The bad guys. You got to be careful. And, by the way, where are they?"

"They went down to get ice cream. Angie went to call them. I'll split mine with you. They should be back any minute."

Just as predicted, the bevy of teenagers returned. Hamish's ice cream was in a little pink cup with a plastic top, tucked in a white polka dotted bag. "I got you two spoons, because I thought Mom might want to share, but—"

"I'll share with Harper. If Mom didn't want one when you left, she won't want one now. Thanks, Sasha. Everybody good?"

"We are. Are you going to stay out here very much longer?" she asked.

"I was just about to get out. I was thinking of taking a swim. Why?" Hamish noticed the look on some of the kids' faces went sad.

Cora was brave enough to describe the obvious. "They wanted to kind of take over the pool, play some music, games, dance, and stuff. Would you mind if we had some privacy?"

Hamish and Harper exchanged the look. "Cora, that's not nice."

"Dad, either way is fine with us."

Hamish's two sons were standing next to her with wrinkled noses. He knew they weren't excited about it.

"Nah, I'm good. Harper and I are going to go inside and pig out on this ice cream. Don't stay out too late. We don't want to bother the neighbors, either. I want you to make sure to get to bed before nine o'clock, okay?"

"Roger that," answered Sasha.

CHAPTER 2

ANGIE McDOUGALL HAD been enjoying Hamish being home these past five months. His recovery and PT had been going well, and she appreciated the fact that he was around more for the kids, who seemed to always hang on him. Because he was the celebrity of the family, she took it in stride and didn't want to interfere with his quality time with the kids. She didn't mind all the attention on him.

It was also nice he could take care of a few things around the house he couldn't do when he was gone for overseas deployment. She felt a huge burden lift from her shoulders. She hated talking to auto mechanics, plumbers, or pool maintenance people, but she did it, nonetheless. But it was nice now to have backup. They all listened to Hamish more than they did her, so it was even more effective.

In short, it was nice being around him, having their toes touch in the mornings and at night, having coffee with him on the back deck, just being a regular husband and wife. One of their friends told her, "You just have to bump into each other a whole bunch of times to keep that friendship, that love going."

And it was true. Angie needed the "stick around time" with him now that he was home, doing little things like putting away the dishes or loading the dishwasher or washing the never-ending laundry a family of six generates. Even folding clothes together was a celebration of ordinary life she loved. She appreciated him taking the car down to get gassed up or washed. It helped create the glue in their marriage she hadn't realized was missing. She was reluctant to have this change now that he was healthy and ready to deploy again.

Hamish had plans to take the boys camping, which they had missed for over two years. On several of his latest deployments before he switched over to the Silver Team, he came back banged up and sometimes with broken bones or torn ligaments. It took him several weeks to recover, and he wasn't able to be active with them, playing football or soccer, taking the camping trip or horseback riding. Yet the boys weren't getting any younger, and they missed these times with their dad. They missed everything about him. They missed his good days and his bad days.

With luck, he'd have enough time to do a couple of

things before he deployed. But now, with the visit from Harper, she wasn't sure.

Angie knew Hamish missed these things too. For these five blessed months, she finally had Hamish almost all to herself. The man continually surprised her. He'd exceeded all her expectations. Sadly, these days would now be coming to an end.

She and her best friend, Marie Brown, married to a former Team 3 guy who served with Harper, even found time to go shopping for school clothes, as well as do a little bit of recreational beauty things like getting their toes and nails done and getting facials or massages together. It was something she hadn't been able to afford to do before, and now with the extra income Hamish was making, she could luxuriate in a few of these things.

Marie was a small woman, very athletic, a sprinter but still a marathon runner. She liked the challenge of the different headspaces and pacing required for each. She and her husband had no children, so she threw herself into her distance running and soccer. She went to college playing soccer, almost made the US Olympic Team, and now coached a number of developmental girls' teams down in the very competitive San Diego area.

In Hamish's family, the boys were into soccer big time. Marie sometimes came over and coached them, and she was tough. Sasha played soccer, but the girls primarily wanted to play volleyball or basketball. Hamish was able to help a little bit with both, since he played both men's beach volleyball and basketball in his brief college stint.

Marie was the best friend a girl could ever have, more like a true sister to Angie. A member of the family. She didn't feel the same way about Marie's husband, Connor.

"How's he doing today?" Marie asked her.

"Oh, you mean the king of good times?" Angie asked.

"That's him. The king. The king of good times, the king of all times, right?"

"You're so right. Just found out he's going to be deploying soon. His boss came over to check him out. I'm sure they'll ask for a doctor sign off, but Hamish has been doing great."

"He has. A remarkable recovery, Angie."

"I've never seen him be able to be so patient with the kids, relax and sit back. It's just been a wonderful summer and early fall. I kind of hate for it to end, but you know what they say."

"Of course. All things must come to an end some-day. But somehow you and I think differently, don't we, Angie? We like to mess with the odds."

"That's why I love you, Marie. That's why I need to

see you every day. You keep my spirits up."

"Why? Is something out of whack?" she asked.

"Everything's fine. I just don't like change. I like him home. I like him with us. And I tell him that all the time. Now he's starting to ask me 'why, you don't want me to go back?' You know, all those questions are popping up. You understand how it is. We don't want to tell him we'd much rather they not have such a dangerous job, because we don't want to affect their decisions. It's their decision."

"Well, Angie, the longer we're married, and I don't have to tell you this after thirty years, the more you realize that it's really a joint decision, isn't it? You want them to be happy with what they're doing. You just wish there was a way they could do it without putting their lives on the line every day. At first when Connor left the teams, it was a tough couple of years for him, even though I was relieved. I even felt guilty for it. Worried that I'd caused it. And wondered if this was what he really wanted."

"I remember those times. It was tough, I know."

"I honestly thought we'd have a lot more long-term problems than we did."

"And then he got that new consulting job he loves, right?"

"He's closed lipped about it, but yes, that helped. The extra income certainly helped us adjust."

"How is Connor's work going? Still the dream job or can you say?"

"He seems to be enjoying it. Some days, I'm not sure. He worries more. It's all mental stress, not the physical stress on the Teams. I think these men of action have a hard time adjusting to desk jobs, even if it is consulting on things they know a great deal about. Former SEALs are always in demand everywhere. But it wasn't what he was trained to be the best at. And he has to work with a lot of people who don't have the same ethics or dedication. I think he liked the tightness of the Teams better, but he says this is right for him, so I'm standing behind that."

"Who does he consult for?"

"I'm not supposed to say. Some corporate entities, people in the defense industry, companies who work for the Feds, and some political committees. He does research and background reports for the group he works for. Always something new coming down the line. We'll see."

"Does he have any interest in joining the Silver Team?"

"At one time he did. Not sure now."

"He should talk to Hamish, then. They're friends too, right?"

"I don't think they talk much. But I really don't know. I think he'd fit right in, so maybe I'll mention it to him. Thanks for reminding me."

"Good to have some kind of option in case it doesn't work out. I know Harper is always looking for new talent."

"He does like being part of a Team. He likes being support. He says he does this now, just that they're not on the battlefield. He's working with other consultants, giving support to those that do work overseas, specialized contractors. Not all attached to military. But I think he works with the Navy the most."

"They really should talk, Marie."

"I have to be careful. I've probably already said too much, so keep it close, okay?"

"Well, as long as he's doing what he wants, making a contribution, it doesn't matter the form. I know he wants to still forward serve. Hamish and Harper feel the same way."

"Yes, the way Connor put it, sometimes they need really good actionable information from people who have not just been bureaucrats but actually been in the field, so I think Connor has been good with that. SEAL Team 3 did a lot of ops on human trafficking on their deployments. He told me that's what the Silver Team will be focusing on next."

"Well, Marie, you know more than I do, it seems." Angie was surprised this information had spread. She'd thought it was a closely guarded secret. So she had to ask.

"Human trafficking? He's working on that now too?"

Marie was hesitant to answer. "Yes, and I better stop there. I really don't know everything about it. He told me last night."

"More intelligence is key. I know Hamish used to complain when they'd get into pickles overseas when the intelligence was spotty or, worse, inaccurate. It's so important."

Angie didn't want to pry further, and she was already burdened with a secret from Marie she wasn't comfortable agreeing to, so she changed the subject.

She handed Marie the soccer uniforms she'd washed and folded for her. "Here you go. Now I have to get ready for dinner. But thanks for a great day. I always enjoy spending time with you."

"Me too."

They hugged. Now Angie was stuck with a dilemma. Should she keep her word to her friend, or should she mention this conversation to Hamish?

It didn't take long for her cobwebs of guilt to blow away. Of course, she'd always give her biggest loyalty to Hamish. She just wished she didn't have to go against a friend.

And, Angie, maybe you're making too much of this, she thought, and switched it off to prepare for dinner. The troops would be home soon, eating her out of house and home.

CHAPTER 3

HARPER CUNNINGHAM ASKED Hamish to accompany him to a special meeting with Admiral Patterson and President Collier in D.C.. She walked in on him packing.

"You'll be back tomorrow?" Angie asked him.

"Yup. You have plans?"

"No, just wondering. I have a couple of things I wanted to talk to you about, but it can wait until you get back."

"You sure?" Hamish asked, hugging her tight. "I've got time now."

"No, I don't want to clutter your head with it now. Not important. It's not life-threatening."

"Now you're being mysterious."

"No. Honest. If it was important, I'd talk to you about it. Besides, I'm not even sure it's worth talking about. You just have a good meeting. I'm glad you're spending time with Harper, and how exciting to meet the president again."

"He's one of the good guys, Angie. I like working for them. I really do."

She dropped him off at the Silver Team building on base.

Admiral Patterson had sent a sleek black private jet for the two of them. They sat side-by-side sipping a modest amount of American whiskey.

"Don't want to show up drunk to the boss, you know?" Hamish said.

"We're not gonna see him till 0800, but yeah, I get it. One is enough. For old times, Hamish?" said Harper.

They clinked their glasses.

"Yeah, boy, you think of all the years we worked together, even when we worked on other teams, there's lots of history there. We saw each other at weddings and funerals and everything in between. I was getting used to working with you again on the Silver Team... then my surgery. So sorry I wasn't ready for the last mission."

"Not your fault. You got yourself righted. That's the main thing. Now, don't go getting injured on the next run, or I might say something about it."

Hamish laughed and sipped.

Harper slapped him on the knee. "I'm seriously glad you're by my side in this endeavor. It's still kind of new, and I'm not twenty years old anymore. And who knew I'd be actually running a Team?"

"That's a good sign. Means you're growing as a leader, Harper. That's what you want. We all have to be learning new things every time we go out. Part of our SEAL training, right?"

"Abso-fuckin'-lutely."

"And, as far as being helpful, I've got a gut, and I'm easily forty pounds overweight, but I can still bench press eighty percent of what I used to, and I can still caber toss. I just don't think I can throw it as far."

Harper laughed. "Point well taken."

As he thought about it more, he came up with some other revelations. "But sometimes I think that's good. You know when you're young and you think fast and you jump in and you act. You're a man of action. We used to make a lot of mistakes too, Harper."

"But we gutted it out. We just pushed ourselves to the limit, because back then, you were gonna live forever, and we didn't have anybody else to live for, did we?"

"Ain't that the truth. I had Angie by that time, but we didn't start having kids for more than ten years. Sometimes I wish I'd started much sooner. With a young family at home, it makes me afraid to get hurt." He corrected himself. "Not afraid, but you know I think about it."

"Well, look at me, with a newborn and thinking about duplicating her ass!"

Hamish almost spit out his whiskey.

"The good thing is something happens to us, there's a hell of a package coming our family's way. Not that that's a good reason to go run in and do something stupid," Hamish added.

They clinked glasses again. "True that," said Harper. "Did you ever think you'd have such a brood, that you'd be flying in a private jet like this, getting ready to meet with the President of the United States and Admiral Patterson?" Harper asked him.

"Nah, I've never been that kind of a dreamer. I just put one foot in front of the other and take what comes. I think it's because I have all these little orbits around me. I'm managing—well, I don't really manage it, Angie does. She does it so damn well. She keeps all the kids schedules straight, and you know she's the general when I'm gone, and when I come back, I'm Mr. Big Cheese, and she puts me in my place pretty quickly. You know that happens, don't you?"

"I think she probably does it way more lovingly than you want to admit, Hamish. She's a good kid. She's still a good kid at her age. You got lucky there. I only wish I'd found somebody sooner. Found somebody when I was younger. She got to see you and your giant Olympian phase, right?"

"No to the Olympics, that was never going to be my thing. The best thing I could do was toss a telephone pole and impress the guys at BUD/s when I did it. Nobody believed me. I think I'm the only one."

"Hate to break it to you, Sport, but I think that record's been broken a few times, Hamish. But I'm not saying a word."

They both laughed again.

Hamish looked through the window out at the white and peachy colored clouds that were now fading into deep gray as they headed through the time zones and into night time. He thought the whiskey would help him catch a little nap, but it wasn't to be. After about an hour, he moved to the seat across from Harper so he could stretch his legs, and Harper could do the same. Adjusting the chair backward, he leaned against the side of the plane and the window, looking at the forever horizon and then the darker sky approaching and, finally, the twinkling lights in the distance.

All kinds of images popped through his head. The kids running around and in the pool, the ice cream he and Harper shared in the house after they got back, the way Angie lovingly oiled down his knee and both thighs every night, which of course turned into a sexual escapade, leaving both of them oily and desperate for more.

He smiled at his sweet life. His sweet wife. She was still his gal, always was and always would be. There were a lot of happy memories in their years together, and he couldn't wait to grow old with her. He only hoped that he died before she did, because he wouldn't be able to stand life without her.

They landed. A black Suburban was waiting for them at the private airstrip, taking them to their accommodations.

The Navy had one whole wing of The Ascension Hotel, one of those residences that had no sign and guests had to be somebody to stay there. It wasn't like someone could walk in off the street and just pick a room, grab a date, and have a fling there. It was only for dignitaries, special invitees, or people who needed extra security. Since they were guests of the president, they were treated enormously well. Hamish didn't think even the admiral had enough clout to put them up there.

After their valet showed them to the two-bedroom suite, each with their own white terrycloth bathrobes, each with separate bath with a soaking tub which Hamish was delighted about, they came back together in the living room and raided the mini bar.

"I thought you said only one?" asked Hamish.

"Fuck it, Hamish. We're sitting here in this beautiful suite. Look at the view of the Capitol Building from here for chrissakes! I mean, when I come usually I don't get something like this. They put me up at a regular hotel. But this—this is amazing. I'm celebrating, aren't you?"

"Long as we get up in time. We have to meet him at eight?" Hamish asked.

"0800. We should leave around 7:30. That's when I told the car to show up downstairs. If we want breakfast, we should preorder it now."

Hamish looked over the paper menu that was left on the desk showing a huge list of American and international breakfasts, everything from miso soup to steak and eggs. It was a lavish spread. All at the government's expense. Hamish felt somewhat guilty. But he couldn't leave cheese grits and strawberry blintzes alone. He was going to have to order and sample everything: pancakes and blintzes, the grits, corn muffins, orange marmalade, and a huge pot of coffee along with a carafe of fresh squeezed orange juice. He was getting hungry just thinking about it.

"I think I just charged a $200 breakfast to the president's account." Hamish chuckled.

"Don't worry about it. I think he can afford it."

IN THE MORNING, they were ushered into Admiral Patterson's media room, which contained a huge circular table that could easily seat thirty people. On two of the walls, maps of the world hung, along with whiteboards and other maps and charts that were rolled up and stowed above. It was a full-on briefing room, better than anything they'd ever seen on the Teams.

Hamish sat down and felt the cushy leather chair squeak beneath him, halfway thinking the whole thing was going to collapse.

"Watch it there, Hamish. They might make you pay for that if you break it," added Harper.

"I think it's all the pancakes and muffins. I think I drank all that coffee too, man. I've got to pee. I'm about to spring a leak from several orifices. I might close down this whole wing with a strange odor, Harper. Can I go do that first, if it won't get me canned?"

"Sure. Just pop your head out the door there, and somebody will show you the right way. There's no chance they're gonna let you wander around. You look too dangerous."

That was funny.

As he opened the door, he turned around to face Harper, giving him a wicked grin, showing off his canines. Wiggling his eyebrows, he made it out to the hallway and closed the door behind him.

Admiral Patterson entered about five minutes later, before Hamish was back.

"Where is your cohort?" he asked.

"Went to go take a leak, sir. I'm going to have to follow him next but didn't want to leave the room vacant for you."

Just then Hamish arrived. "Sir?" Hamish said as he shook Admiral Patterson's hand.

"Nice to meet you again, Hamish."

"I'm going to be right back," Harper said as he dove out the door.

Patterson began. "I'm really glad you're part of the Team. I know I told you that after our first mission, and I'm sorry you missed the second one. How's the knee?"

"Oh, it's better than it's ever been. I've been suffering with that thing over twenty years from my rugby injury. But first time was just a shit job. This one, I got first class treatment, and I think I got the best orthopedic surgeon, specializing in knees and hips, in the whole West Coast. My leg works better than a machine, and there's no clicking sounds, no pain, no nothing. And I'm actually starting to enjoy sleeping."

"Good to hear. You know you're lucky you didn't get addicted. A lot of guys survive their injury but get hooked on the pills and then wash out. It's a real shame. I'm really glad that didn't happen to you."

"No, I've never been one to take drugs. I tried to duke it out. Now a whisky or two, well, that's a different story. And I've been known to down quite a bit of that. But no, I don't like those painkillers. Only take them when I have to and just for the first few days."

Harper arrived back in the room.

"Sorry, sir, big breakfast this morning. I guess my body is not used to it," he said. He took a seat next to Hamish.

"Well, gents, let me begin. The president always runs late. I'm on a tight schedule today."

The two of them sat to attention, waiting for the mission briefing.

"We've got ourselves a human trafficking ring that has just gotten real nasty. As you know, the president almost sees it as his personal mission to eradicate this scourge—a very lofty and noble goal. But he's authorized a commission to prepare a report on it, and you'll get copies. We had to do this under great secrecy, and you'll learn why in a moment."

Hamish was delighted President Collier felt so strongly about the subject, as he did.

"I don't think I need to tell you this whole criminal enterprise is worldwide and is getting worse. There are so many countries around the globe that don't respect women and children, and there are elements in our own society that feel it's their right to abuse the less fortunate as well, not something I'm very proud of. You have a class of people with money, and you have people who need protection, and it's a deadly combination when the two meet."

"Couldn't agree more," said Harper.

"That's the state of things, sir," said Hamish.

"When somebody can't stop an abuser, or we have to count on their better angels to stop or regulate themselves, and they never can, we have a bad situation. When they make it their own criminal enterprise, making money off the misery of the poor and the vulnerable, well, it's the highest form of evil out there."

"We're both with you, sir," said Harper.

"I'm just sick of the whole thing, but the president, who will be joining us shortly, is especially taking this on. He may run on that platform going forward, so this has bigger implications far down the road."

"Understood, sir," said Hamish.

"Well, from what we've seen, Hamish and I, and we saw the point of origin for a lot of these mostly girls and young children, it's just hell on earth. Dreams dashed. It's sickening to us as well. So you tell us what we need to do, and we'll go get it done, sir," said Harper.

Admiral Patterson looked between the two men. "The slave trade has been around for thousands of years, since the dawn of man. Now we can't even call it that because it's too sensitive of a word to use. Ridiculous! We like to think that our sophisticated modern civilization would have grown up, but as long as there's a buck to be made, and in this case, there's lots of money to be made, there's really no way to stop it. But we got a line on a group of—"

Just then the president arrived. Hamish and Harper began to stand.

"No, stay seated, gentlemen," President Collier said. "We're going to keep this as informal as we can."

Hamish re-took his seat.

"And by the way, welcome." He leaned across the table and shook both of their hands. Then he took a seat next to Admiral Patterson.

"I was just about to explain to him what we've uncovered."

"So let me do it then, and it's a short and sweet tale. As you know, our southern border is rife with human trafficking, and we've tried to stamp it out. We've tried to do everything we can. It's impossible to infiltrate the groups, although we've tried that as well and lost men in the process. Unfortunately, San Diego and most of Southern California are hot beds of activity since we have a long coastline and the possibility of arriving by sea or air. And we add the factor that we have the close proximity to Las Vegas. That's the magnet for a lot of these girls coming through here."

Hamish wasn't aware of this connection.

"And, thanks to a confidential informant, we've just discovered a very dangerous group, not a new one, but one that has been operating under the radar for a few years now, run by an NGO our government has trusted to safely take care of some of the migrant placement and tracking. We partner with several of these, because the problem is so massive it's too big for us to handle and, frankly, probably not something we'd manage a very good job of doing. Which means things slip by undetected."

Hamish waited for the short and sweet part. He hoped it was coming, because he had to use the bathroom again.

Admiral Patterson added his comment next. "Gentlemen, this information has to stay in this room, only between us. We've done the study, hopefully under complete secrecy. But you know it's hard to keep things a secret in this town, even with hand-picked special agents who have worked tirelessly to bring forward this report. The president has really stuck his neck out here to get to the root cause of all this evil. This is highly sensitive, classified information. Lives are at stake, including yours and your families."

Hamish paid attention to every expression the two men made. He saw worry and doubt there. This wasn't going to be a picnic.

The president put the cherry on top.

"Our sources have led us to a group run by several elected officials, unfortunately. We have several agencies and jurisdictions involved. We got one sheriff, six mayors, and one U.S. Senator that we know of. More coming. All on the payroll of some of the most powerful cartels from Mexico, with international funding. This is going to be messy. There's going to be a huge amount of resistance. These people won't go down without a fight, and they won't be concerned about collateral damage, so you're going to have to be very careful. We're tasking a small group from here as support, including an FBI special agent and others of the president's personal staff, who are vetted and dedicated to his vision of change."

Before Hamish could figure out what his stomach was telling him, President Collier leaned into the table.

"I'm not even sure if it isn't too late. But, one by one, I want to clean out all these rats. It's going to be extremely dangerous, and at times, you aren't going to know who friend or foe is."

"May I ask your confidential source?" asked Harper.

Patterson looked to the president, who continued, "He's a priest. Father Flaherty, in Arizona, works for the Archdiocese out of Phoenix, specializing in helping migrants find placement. But he's just found out that his real job is helping to facilitate a large NGO, a front for a criminal enterprise, funneling dark money, called the Indigenous Peoples Project."

Harper gasped. "You talking about infiltration of the Indian tribes?"

"No, not actively. We think they are unwilling accomplices. It's been well documented the Navajo have had a problem with this for decades—girls being kidnapped and winding up in Las Vegas or never found again."

"But run by a senator?" Harper insisted. "Father's a dead man," he whispered.

"Yes, we understand that. That is also why part of your mission is to keep that man alive. We've just completed his witness protection agreement. He's agreed to help us all he can, and once we're done, he will be placed through them. But we need him to stay in place for now, and he's agreed to do so, until we get the roundup and evidence we need to shut them down. It is also going to be extremely important we do everything we can to keep him safe."

Hamish could understand the courage this priest was demonstrating. Harper was right. His odds were long, but Hamish vowed to protect that man with his life. Harper did too.

"I want you to meet with him. He's at a conference in San Diego for the next three days. I'm giving you his direct contact number, and he's expecting a call from you. When you get back, make sure you meet him in person. He's got answers for most of your questions.

He's got concerns and questions of his own as well."

"Consider it done," said Harper.

The president gave Harper a piece of paper and a card. "My personal number in case you need something in an emergency," he said. "This is how to reach Flaherty. You'll be getting a ton of things sent by secure server. I want you to read it all over if you can before you meet with him. I need you two up to speed."

"Thank you for your trust and faith in us, sir," Harper said, taking the paper and card.

"Let me remind you, none of this can be left where anyone else will see it. You can't discuss it even with your wives. I know you know the drill, but no specifics. These reports cannot get outside of our circle or it will bring us all down. Please guard these things with your life."

"Understood. We won't let you down, Mr. President," said Hamish.

As they left for their suite to pack up and get to the airport, the low-level panic in the back of his head bothered him. What was the cost going to be for him doing this? Would this affect Angie and the kids?

The only answer was: *of course it will*. So the task was also to get them prepared to face the pits of hell, for him to keep them safely out of the way.

It was the most dangerous job he'd ever undertaken. He hoped he was man enough to handle it.

CHAPTER 4

ANGIE WAS WAITING for Hamish to arrive home from Washington D.C.. Her mother's birthday was coming up, and she was looking for some great photos of the kids she could have printed and put into frames to gift her. She knew Sasha had taken several recent pictures of them at the pool, in the hot tub, in huge water fights, and even pictures of the whole family. Noticing her phone was left on the dining room table, she picked it up and started scrolling through Sasha's photos.

It didn't occur to her that Sasha would have a problem with it, since she wasn't checking messages or looking for anything nefarious. She was just searching for family photos. In hindsight, she should've thought about it first.

All of a sudden, she found several photos of what appeared to be a youth, judging from the look of him, from the lower abdomen down to his mid-thigh, exposing his groin. The teen was naked. There were four shots, all of them different angles. In one of them, he was using his right hand to masturbate.

Her heart sank as fear gripped her. She didn't know whether to scream or cry. Her heart began pounding in her chest, anger swelling, exploding, ready to take over her whole body. Sasha had been violated with these photos sent. In turn, she, Angie, felt violated.

She was coming to grips with what she'd seen when she heard Sasha bounding down the stairs. Instinctively, she put the phone behind her back, as if she wanted to hide it from her teenager.

"Mom, have you seen my phone?"

Angie pulled Sasha's phone from behind her back and held the screen up to her face. "This one, you mean?"

Her reaction was immediate. "Mother!" Sasha's face became disfigured into a horrible, hateful scowl. She turned bright red and then immediately burst into tears. She was clearly out of her mind. "You have no right!" she screamed.

"What do you mean I don't have the right, Sasha? Who sent these?"

"You've invaded my private space! You—"

Angie cut her off. "This is against the law, Sasha. These are awful pictures. Someone sent these to you. I can't tell who it is. Who sent them?"

"So you have the right now to censure my photos, and are you checking my messages too?"

"Should I be?"

"Mother! Of course not! Are you insane?" She stomped back and forth. "I can't believe you'd do something like this."

"Me? How about the asshole who did this?" She held the phone up to her again.

"Give me that. It isn't yours."

Angie held the phone behind her back again. "Young lady, you're fourteen years old, and you live in our house. I have a right to know if someone is sending you sexual pictures. This is not right, Sasha. This is so far from right it isn't funny."

"So now you're going to be the judge of what I can see and not see? Mom, this is no big deal. I've seen worse."

"Oh, really? Where?"

"Oh, come on. I read, I watch TV, and I go to the movies. This is tame compared to the things I've seen."

"That's interesting. Where are you seeing things like this? This is sick, Sasha. Pure sickness. Do you know this boy?"

"No. I have no idea who sent them. You're blaming me for something I didn't do. Someone else did. Not me. Are you going to restrict what comes to my phone, who I can see, talk to? Am I going to even be allowed to breathe in this house?"

Angie stepped toward her daughter and almost slapped her across the face. She certainly felt like doing it but held back at the last minute. She calmed her voice. It took real effort.

"I want an explanation. This is dangerous, Sasha. Are you sending pictures of yourself to this person? And is this somebody from school?"

"It's probably just a prank, one of the boys at school. I mean, obviously, you can see it's a kid right? Not some creepy old man."

"And you think that makes this okay?"

"No, I'm not saying that, but—"

"How do you know it's not from some creepy old man?" asked Angie.

Sasha was trying to compose herself, but she was still shaking. She wiped tears streaming down her face.

"It's not anything you should be concerned about, Mom."

"How in God's name is that so?"

"Because, it's happened to other girls in my class. It's a thing now that some of the guys do at school. They get together, and they get your phone number— we give our phone numbers out all the time. We text stuff about homework and all sorts of stuff—you've seen me do it."

"Yes, I have. But this is different, Sasha."

"It's just this thing they do. They get together at somebody's house, and they do these dumb things. They get a burner phone so it doesn't show who they really are. I know it's creepy, and I don't know who it is, but I don't want to get them in trouble. They might be friends of mine."

"Get them in trouble? This is against the law. It's not anything they should do for a prank. What friend of yours would ever do something like that and is this person who did this—is this person really a friend of yours?"

"No, Mom. I don't think any of my friends would do that, really. Maybe someone from school, though. A friend of a friend. It's just some random jerk trying to get some laughs at my expense, that's all."

"That's all? Would you listen to yourself, Sasha!" Angie was beginning to get more and more agitated.

"Look, I get that you're upset, but I didn't cause this. That person did it. He just picked me to play the prank on. I'm not going to make a federal case out of it, and I don't want you to either."

Angie had to sit down. Still holding the cell phone, she put her face into her hands, and this time it was her turn to cry. She could not believe how casual her daughter was to all of this.

Then she looked back at the distress in her daughter's face. Angie felt she'd let Sasha down, that she'd not properly forewarned her about this type of thing, and she was struggling under the guilt. After the anger left, there was tremendous guilt. Her daughter was left more vulnerable due to her inattention and lack of taking proper precautions.

Sasha sat beside her. "Mom. You're getting overly worked up over nothing. I don't know who it is, honest. If I did, I'd tell you. But no one I know of would ever do this. We pass our numbers around a lot, and it's happened to other people. We just ignore it and go on. I mean, if we make a big deal about it, then all of a sudden, we get outed. All the kids begin to tease you, and in one case, one of my friends started getting hundreds of pictures after she complained to the school counselors. Whoever started it just ratcheted it up, and then she finally had to get rid of her phone and change her phone number, and they got the police involved."

"As they should have. Why didn't I ever hear anything about this?"

"Because it happened at St. John's. It wasn't at my school. The Catholic school. She's on my volleyball team. They took a hard stance on this sort of thing, and there was an all-school assembly, and, oh my gosh, my friend was so embarrassed. She wished she'd never said anything about it. The boys started teasing her for being afraid of sex or being a prude. It was terrible. The family is considering transferring to another school. Now she's going to lose all her friends."

"Well, obviously there's more than one way to handle it, and I am not sure about all the details, but why am I just hearing about this, and how come you didn't tell me when you got these? You know this is wrong."

"Because honestly, I don't think it's any big deal. If you want, I'll just erase them."

"No, Sasha, I'm going to keep your phone. I need this to show your dad."

"Oh, come on! You can't do that. He's going to blow a gasket. I'll be grounded for a year. He'll go all commando on the principal, all the teachers. I don't want a scene. He scares half the parents, anyway."

Angie had heard the same said before. It was the only bit of lightness to their conversation. The King of Good Times could certainly cut a swath.

"But if it's not your fault, Sasha, why would he ground you for a year? Besides, it's not your choice. We're the parents. We get a say in how this is handled."

"I don't want to be punished for something I didn't do."

"You're not being punished. You're being protected. How are we to get to the bottom of it?"

"But, Mom, it's just what teenagers do these days,

and honestly, I think you're getting all worked up over nothing."

"Well, we'll see. I'm going to keep your phone for now. If it will make you feel any better, I have a free one I got for signing up for the gym membership. I haven't activated it yet. It may not have all the features, but it will give you a phone to use for now. And I'm not here to search your messages or look into your personal life at all. Or do you have something to hide, Sasha? Are you involved in this at all?"

"Of course not. You'll find all my texting very boring, Mom. Honest. I think you and Dad text the sexy stuff."

"Sasha!"

She shrugged. "Sorry, Mom. We see your phones blow up sometimes. Hard not to read the messages. We weren't born yesterday!"

"But have you sent pictures of yourself, naked pictures I'm talking about? Or do you know anyone who has?"

"No. We don't do that. If somebody's phone gets hacked and if I've sent a photo or something or posted something online, anybody could take those pictures and use them. It's all public access. As far as this goes, like I said, Mom, it's happened to several of my girlfriends. And it seems to be happening more and more. I looked at them, and then I just decided to talk about it with some of my friends, but I should've just erased them."

"Actually, you did the right thing by saving them. And I am going to have to have a talk with your dad, and I'll see what he thinks we should do."

She put her hands on Sasha's shoulders then rubbed her daughter's cheek with her right hand. "Sasha, sweetheart, we only want to keep you safe. Nobody's saying this is any reflection on you, and I understand about the embarrassment and not wanting to be called out for something like this. I would be horrified if I were your age, so I get it. But there are evil people out there that do awful things, and I am concerned, especially now, in this day and age of all this human trafficking going on, that somebody has gotten access to your personal information. We have to be very careful about that. We want to protect you. This is how predators and stalkers—people of this ilk— operate. That's why they don't get caught sometimes, because people overlook it. They underestimate it, think it's harmless."

Angie held up the phone again.

"Trust me, this is not harmless."

Sasha stormed off to her room. Angie was trying to recall where she put that extra phone and decided she'd wait until Hamish got home before looking any farther.

Now she had two things to talk to him about.

Roughly two hours later, Hamish walked through the door, grabbed her, picked her up, and gave her a big hug and kiss. He seemed overly gentle and protective. Angie figured the trip was long and the mission was complicated. She felt his mind racing, his heart exploding. She was worried about him.

"I'm so glad you're home, Hamish."

He could read her very well. "Something wrong? I was kind of expecting something a little warmer," he said.

"I need you to sit down for a minute before the rest of the kids come home."

Hamish sat next to her on the living room couch. She took the phone from her pocket and handed it to Hamish, finding the picture she wanted to show him.

"This is what I found on Sasha's phone today."

He grabbed the phone as if he was going to crush it between his fingers. He peered at the images. A low rumble emanated in his chest.

In a whisper, he said, "Fuck me. Who did this?"

"I have no idea, and she doesn't either. She thinks it's some guy from school. She says that several of the other girls have also had the same thing happen. She thinks it's just the boys at the school, not one of her friends, that somehow got her number."

"Looks like it was done by a kid, but might be anybody. Somebody could've paid somebody to do this.

Could be some crusty old pervert. Or a pro. These guys don't play by any rules. She said there are more that have had this happen?"

"Yes. And apparently at St. John's, they had a big issue about this, and I've never heard anything, but they had a school assembly about it. One of the girls getting pictures somehow got her name leaked, and instead of getting a few awful pictures like this, she started getting hundreds of them. Sent by several boys in the community, or so they think. She was so embarrassed her parents are considering transferring."

"But did they catch the guy?"

"I guess police couldn't."

"This girl, she's a friend of Sasha's?"

"She plays on the same volleyball team. I'm not sure who she is, but we can find out. Sasha's upstairs. She's expecting you."

"I'm on it." He took two steps in the direction of the stairway then stopped and turned to face her. "Is this what you wanted to talk to me about before I left? Because—"

"No, that's something else. But you go upstairs and talk to her first, and we'll talk about the other one later. It's not nearly as urgent. I told her she couldn't have this phone back until we were done looking at it and maybe giving it to the police. I have an extra phone I got as a signing bonus for the gym membership, if you remember?"

"Yeah, I remember that."

"I told Sasha she can have that phone, except I can't find it."

"I know where it is. But first, we're gonna talk about this. And I'm glad you told her you were keeping it. I want a full forensic analysis on this."

"And, Hamish, just so you know before you go up there, fourteen-year-olds are complicated, and you can't treat her like you can talk to one of your guys on the Team, right?"

"Oh, I get it. I understand. But I'm not gonna mess around with this, Angie. If you want me to be gentle and calm about it, I'm not calm. I'm fucking pissed off as all get out. I'm not gonna rest until I find the son of a bitch who did this. And I don't care if he's a fourteen-year-old kid or the creepy sixty-year-old guy. We're gonna find that asshole. I won't stop until we find him."

"I get that, and I don't disagree. However, she feels her privacy has been violated."

He stepped back into the room. "So some jerk sends her masturbation photos, and she feels violated because we want to know about it? No, that's not good logic, Angie. She's been violated by somebody else, not us. And us trying to get to the bottom of it and protect her, there's nothing wrong with that, and I'm sorry if she gives me a bunch of lip about it. I'm not gonna have any of that."

"Hamish, just listen to me. Please, do it respectfully. I think she feels partially responsible for this."

"Well, that's a whole other story, isn't it? Because if she is, I'm putting an end to it."

"If you want to continue to have a relationship with your daughter, even though you're right, you need to listen to me. You need to have this conversation in such a way that she understands that you love her, that she's not wrong, and that you're her protector. And that you'd do anything to achieve that goal. Just like if it happened to me or Cora. We do need to get to the bottom of it and we will, but say it from that perspective."

"I'll do my best. You may have to come in and do triage afterwards. But dammit, we think we handle all the dangerous things out there, tell them to be careful, and then something like this happens and you find out about it by *accident*. What would've happened if it had gone on for months or years? These things always start this way. We see it more and more."

"Hamish, I've said my peace. You go up there and see what you can do. And you let me know if you need my help."

Hamish had the phone in his right hand while he pounded up the stairs two at a time. His huge frame rattled the windows of the house. She heard him knock on Sasha's door and Sasha's timid response. "Come in, Dad."

Now there was one more thing Angie had to worry about. This one was big. This one made her conversation with Marie miniscule in comparison. Their innocent family life had suddenly become something touched by evil. The question now was if it was a prank or the tip of an iceberg.

CHAPTER 5

H AMISH WAS STIFF and slightly sore when he woke up, since he'd missed his nightly soak in the hot tub last night. He'd had a horrible time falling asleep after his talk with Sasha. At one point, he was so irritated he considered going downstairs after midnight, giving a call to Harper, or having that soak, hoping it would calm his nerves and allow sleep to come. He was on edge and couldn't shake it.

Doing his timed breathing exercises and meditation focusing on relaxation helped and eventually worked. But he'd struggled with it for several hours and woke up not feeling as refreshed as he wanted.

But it also helped him get a clear vision of what it was that was bothering him. He decided that this morning he was going to sit with Angie and have a discussion about the upcoming mission, as well as adopting new rules for the kids and their behavior. In light of some of the things he learned in Washington

D.C., he discovered vulnerabilities in their home security and had some suggestions how to counteract it.

It was barely light when he showered, ground coffee, and brought a fresh mug to Angie while she was still sleeping. Sitting on the edge of the bed, he sat the mugs down on the nightstand, bent over, and kissed her. She rolled over on her back, pulled the hair from her face, and smiled up at him.

"This is different, Hamish. Do I smell coffee?" she asked him.

"Only for you, my love," he said as he held up one of the mugs.

Angie adjusted her pillows and sat up, accepting the warm liquid. She closed her eyes, blew over the top of the mug, and then savored it—that very first fresh coffee with half-and-half. "Hmmm. This is lovely."

"Just watching you, sweetheart. I could get used to this myself," he answered.

He touched her mug with his, took a sip, and then settled it back on the table. He stared down at his hands clasped on his lap.

"What is it, Hamish?" Worry lines appeared on her forehead.

"Angie, I decided something last night when I couldn't sleep. I decided we need to talk about a few things. I got a pretty good indication what our new mission is all about. It has implications for our family. It might also even affect our family, as this is a little bit more dangerous than some of the other things we've done. I need to fully disclose a few things, and I can't go into much detail, so you're going to have to trust me."

"I always trust you, Hamish. Tell me what you can. I'm listening."

"We're going after a sophisticated organization, and I can't reveal names or names of people involved. They deal in child prostitution and human trafficking, run under the guise of a seemingly law-abiding NGO that has ties to several high-ranking elected officials. These officials have power, and we've been told to expect there could be some kind of a pushback. We're going to be careful, of course, but I just need to give you fair warning. And especially in light of what we've discovered with Sasha's phone, it just hit home to me last night. I wasn't going to tell you anything but generalities, but now I have to say more than I wanted, because it's warranted. But you have to promise me you'll keep it just between the two of us, okay?"

"Agreed. Absolutely."

"I think we need to come up with a plan for how to handle the kids and perhaps set some rules and boundaries so that we aren't left exposed in some way. These bad guys don't play fair, and families are fair game sometimes. We need to take precautions."

"I don't think you've ever felt like that before on a mission, have you?"

"No, I haven't. It's never come this close to me. But this time, since we live in Southern California, which has been hugely impacted by all this, and where we're going to be focusing some of our attention, there is a faint possibility our paths could cross. I don't want you put in danger. I want you all prepared."

"Should you be doing this?"

She had a point. He'd asked the same thing of himself.

"It's my job, what I was hired to do. I'm just wanting to be very cautious. We're a border state, and we're in San Diego, which is also close to the border. The chances of our family getting involved or affected is greater. So we need to take precautions."

She was not taking it as well as he'd hoped. He needed to let her ask her questions.

"When you say involved, what do you mean?"

"For example, this thing with Sasha's phone, we have to get the kids to agree that if anything like this pops up they will let us know immediately. It could be something much more serious than they think it is. All of us need to adjust our radar so that we immediately pick up on vibes and signals that are going to be perhaps very subtle. But the consequences could be deadly if we're not careful. And what came to me last night was that I haven't properly prepared everybody for this next step. I listened to Sasha, and now I understand. She doesn't have a clue about what's really out there and how dangerous some of these behaviors really could be."

"Did she seem to understand after you'd talked?"

"She did. I think she got it. She was angry at first, and she blames you for not trusting her, but I explained that you had seen these pictures by accident and that you weren't snooping on her at all. You were looking for photos of the family. I know she believes me, and I know you guys will talk, but I'm going to have to get very graphic and honest with all four of the kids. It's for their own protection, and for yours as well."

Hamish could see Angie was worried, that little wrinkle in her forehead making prominent creases. Her eyes were diverted away, not looking directly into his. He told her he didn't want to have to tell them every detail, but he was going to have to reveal things that were going to scare them. He didn't want to hurt them, but he needed to make sure they were prepared.

"Wow. You think it's necessary? Won't it scare them to death?"

"They should be scared. That's exactly the point, Angie."

"Okay. Go on."

"Let me add that your little talk with me last night before I went to speak to Sasha was helpful. It really was. And I'm sorry if I didn't look like I paid attention to you. I was pretty mad, but I kept hearing your words as I was looking at Sasha. You were absolutely right. The relationship with her is far more important than satisfying my anger. I think she really understands that now."

"Thanks for telling me, Hamish. That means a lot to me. You get pigheaded sometimes. I never know how far to draw the line. I don't like to cross you, especially when you're angry, but I didn't want you to do something that would permanently damage your relationship with her. I'm glad it helped. You would've done fine anyway, but I'm glad I could help."

Hamish was grateful Angie was so resilient, that she handled all the strong things about him, the rough edges and loved them smooth with her persistent and constant demonstration of her love and devotion for him. She was his biggest cheerleader, always in his corner, always trusting, letting him lead when it was necessary, but otherwise being strong and firm enough to stand up when she knew it was important. And last night had been very important. He was completely in love with her.

"I don't deserve you, Angie. But I promise I'm

gonna do a better job showing you my appreciation. And listening better. I've got to listen better."

"Hamish, you have so much on your plate, and with the kids going in all different directions with their activities, it's a crazy time right now. It would be different if it was just the two of us alone somewhere, but we have all six of us, and everybody has different wants and needs and communicates in different ways. They're almost adults. I think the hardest thing for me is trying to temper my communication as a mother. I'm trying to treat them less as children and more as the adults they are."

"You do a great job of it. And there's no way I would be able to go off and do these things if you weren't a capable partner at home holding down the fort, taking care of the family. The difference in what we're gonna do this time is I won't be traveling somewhere far away as much as I'll be conducting things mostly out of the Team Building. I'll be taking occasional trips to Nevada, Arizona, or New Mexico, but I won't be clear across the globe or on the other side of the country."

"I get it. So what is it that you think we need to do first?" she asked him.

"I'm gonna share with them some pictures, graphic pictures. I'm going to share what is really going on out there and how young people are trapped into this human trafficking, human slavery organization. That one or two innocent steps can mean the difference between a life of Hell and a life of safety. I need them to be armed. I probably also need to make sure everybody knows how to fire a gun. I need to make sure that everybody is comfortable they have a weapon they can use in case of an emergency, or at least know where the weapons are and how to use them if something should happen. I need to take everyone down to the gun range, spend time there getting them feeling comfortable shooting."

"I agree. I think they'd love it. You know the boys wanted you to take them hunting. They talk about it all the time."

"Yes, and we'll see what we can do about that. I'm also going to deliver her phone to my FBI liaison in San Diego. In this case, I think a thorough forensic analysis of her phone to see if they can discover where the images came from would be helpful. There's no reason to be worried if, in fact, it was truly something internal at the school—not that it's okay, because it's not. And we're going to ask that they investigate. But we need to get into the data first, before the SDPD sees it."

"I understand. You don't trust them?"

"Right now, I'm not sure who to trust. I trust you. I don't even trust the kids, because they're kids. But they need to know what's going on around them. That prepares them just in case something goes wrong."

"I'm in favor. So far, I'm on board, Hamish."

"Knew you would be, sweetheart." He kissed her. "If the forensic analysis can't determine one way or the other, then we have to assume that she's being targeted. And I want them all to think about that—to think about the fact that somebody could be watching them right now, making moves to do something. Watch for people offering rides or a quick pick up and be more aware if they are alone somewhere or found where someone could cause them harm. They must think analytically that way. They don't have to be afraid to walk outside the front door, but they have to think constructively like that in order to be defensive."

"Wow. You're right. We haven't spent any time on that at all, have we?"

"No, and that's my fault, Angie."

"I'm behind you one hundred percent, Hamish. Thank you."

"One of the things that Admiral Patterson told me I should do, and Harper agrees, is get acquainted with Danny Begay, who is on SEAL Team 3. He's still active on Kyle's team. Danny is Native American—Navajo, or the proper term Dine—and he has a lot of experience recognizing signs of trafficking since both he and his wife partially grew up on the Navajo reservation. A high percentage of those girls have been trafficked into sex slavery in Las Vegas. It's been going on for generations but recently has shown a sharp increase with the additional border crossings."

"Good Lord. That's terrible. I didn't know that."

"What's worse, there's some kind of a connection with this NGO involving a faction of the Navajo tribal leadership. They operate under the protection of some highly placed elected officials that are causing the smoke screen that allows them to operate their illegal business. They prey on the innocents. Danny knows a lot about this because of how he was raised, his wife as well. She was a teacher in the Navajo school. They have family and deep roots there, so I'd like to bring them over with their children. They're solid people. We may need their support. I welcome their suggestions. In Luci, especially, you could find an ally in case something comes up and I'm gone."

"Sounds like we should do this soon. How big is their family?"

"They've got three. Danny adopted a little Iraqi boy who became orphaned on one of SEAL Team 3 missions Harper was on. We heard all about this on the Teams, but I'm not so sure the wives heard as much as we did. Danny also is the grandson of a Code Talker that helped the United States win World War II."

"I've heard about the Code Talkers. So Danny's

grandfather was one of those?"

"Yes. He knows the culture, and since it is a huge problem on the reservation, he's familiar with some of the players and some of the ways in which they operate. I have not had any experience with it so I think having them come over and becoming acquainted with our family would be a good idea. I'm gonna request him as a consultant if he's willing."

"Of course. I don't mind at all. Set it up."

"I'm going to lay out some plans, and I think we need to sit them down tonight. All four of them—just like our Team meetings where we're talking about what could happen and how to be prepared and what to look for and who these people are and how they operate. It's the same thing for this family, except I won't get into great detail. I can't divulge certain things, even to you, sweetheart. But part of my task is to keep you all safe, and I promise I will defend that with my life. We are a Team, are we not?"

"Absolutely."

"You guys will help me in my mission if you also know what it is that I'm trying to combat. And our kids are in the community talking to other kids and just like with this phone thing and pictures of kids' privates— that shouldn't be something they think is okay. Those are some of the things we must teach them. And that's what we're gonna have to do."

"I agree. I agree with all of it. No hesitation."

"I'm going to write out some notes. I have to be gone today for a meeting in San Diego with Harper. But let's meet with the family tonight. They need to be free. Can you arrange that?"

"Of course. I'm not aware of anything scheduled, but absolutely."

"Danny and his wife and their kids by maybe next weekend?"

"Like I said, no problem. I think we're free. No tournaments next weekend. You want to invite them, or should I?"

"I want to talk to Danny myself first. I knew you were going to be okay with all of this."

"Hamish, this is me. I'm your wife. I believe in you. I know you wouldn't bring something like this up if you didn't think it was important. I trust you and I trust your experience and your training. And if you say this needs to be done, there's no question it needs to be done. That's it."

Hamish was delighted with her answer. He could also tell from the look she gave him that there was something else on her mind.

"There's one thing I want to tell you while we're on the subject. I know you and Connor Brown are not exactly close, and I've never understood why that was. But Marie told me something that I just thought you should know about. And she asked me not to say anything to you. So I'm violating her trust, but I think it's important."

"Marie and Connor Brown? Something going on with them?" Hamish asked.

"No, not them, It's Connor's job. Apparently, he's doing some consulting, and she was asking me questions about what you did with the Silver Team. I, of course, couldn't say much, and she wouldn't tell me much either, but I got the idea that he's working for some group that somehow is involved in migrant travel, housing, and placement. It's a consultant group that helps legislators decide on bills and what things to pass, gives expertise. SEAL Team 3 has experienced a lot of human trafficking work on their missions, and so I guess Connor was enlisted in this because of his background. But it doesn't sound like it's exactly sanctioned by the Navy, although she says he does work for them. What kind of work could he do?"

"Hard to say. I'll put out some feelers. It doesn't sound right. The Navy doesn't do that, not without some clearance from the Headshed."

"To me, it sounds like it's outside of the military, so I don't quite understand what he's doing. But there's just something about it that's off to me."

"I'll ask Harper and he probably will have some ideas. I don't know that they were close, but they were on the same team. I'll ask him when I talk to him this morning."

"Thanks, Hamish. And again, if you talk to Marie or Connor, please don't mention I said anything."

"My lips are sealed my love. Especially for you."

HARPER AND HAMISH met Father Flaherty at a popular bagel spot off the strand that had a back room groups sometimes used for meetings.

He was dressed in his black frock. Hamish noticed he had a kind face. He hadn't been out in the sun much, but underneath the gowns, he had a strong physique even though he was older than both of them by more than ten years.

He searched around the room nervously, was beginning to show symptoms of a caged animal like they'd seen so many times overseas when informers came forward at risk of putting themselves or their families at risk.

They insisted on sitting facing the doorway, with good access to windows. Harper brought their tray over when their order was called.

"I can't indulge too much these days, but I do love a good bagel and cream cheese, don't you?" he said with a smile.

"Can't pass them up either," agreed Hamish.

They became absorbed in stuffing their mouths

with the goodness of the bagels and various cheese spreads available to them. When they were done, all three had moustaches of cream cheese on them.

"So, Father, first let me tell you that Hamish and I and our team are honored to be working for your protection. We're also working on a plan not unlike what we did overseas, to tighten this net around them and help shut the enterprise down. We've done this many times. With your help, we'll keep you safe. But I have to mention one thing. No matter how scary it gets, and it might, I can't have you bolting out on your own, even though you may want to. We can't protect you if we don't know where you are."

"I understand," he said.

"So the biggest problem is keeping in touch, without alerting anyone who might be watching you."

"Oh, I think they already are."

Hamish and Harper looked to each other.

"Explain, please."

"Only this morning, one of my staff said someone from the company asked him what I did in my spare time. Me, of all people. Probably the most boring person in the world. He warned me because he said it was how it was asked that triggered something in him."

"You trust this staffer?" asked Harper.

"Completely. We've worked together for almost twenty years. He's not a priest, a paid staffer. The church is his life, and he believes in our mission."

"How would you describe that mission, just so we're clear," asked Harper.

"To feed the starving, help the poor, and keep families safe, many of whom are migrants fleeing persecution in their home countries. We are charged with doing what Jesus would do."

"And that's still the mission?" asked Hamish.

"It is. It started that way. And then I began seeing a change. I began dealing with the company, actually several of them. One would come then fold. Another would pop up in its place. But the biggest problem for me was I started getting inquiries from priests in Mexico and Central America, on behalf of families who had never heard from their family members since they left for the U.S.. I used to have access to that placement information and could forward it along, give them some reassurance. But more and more, I couldn't find any record of people I had processed and counseled myself. The more I checked, the less access I had. Now, I need permission to look into a certain database, especially the one with children."

Hamish saw the tears in the priest's eyes. He was filled with pain.

"Gentlemen, there are thousands of children that are simply unaccounted for. I asked my Bishop how I could inquire, and he told me not to say anything, that oversight was happening and not to worry. Unfortunately, the church ministry is partially funded by these organizations. To question them might jeopardize our own ability to do the good work priests and friends of the church are trying to do. Our team is made up of spiritual patriots—we want to save people."

He looked down at his folded hands on the table.

"Not process them into oblivion."

"Is your Bishop someone you can count on?" asked Harper.

"Sadly, I don't think so. Have you heard the expression 'Money speaks louder than the heart?'"

Harper thought about what they'd been told. He explained that Flaherty needed to gather a list of definite people he could trust and get that list to them. He asked that he try to give him an organizational map of all the players, who he was certain of and who he didn't trust. And also mark definite bad actors and why.

"How will I get this to you?"

"If we get you a computer, could you do it on there in your room? Send us the files? That way, there'd be no paperwork, nothing obvious. We could get something like we use overseas with encryption, impossible to hack."

"I already have a computer," he said.

"Not like what we're going to give you. You have a

Mac?"

"Yes, I do. Macbook Pro 13 inch."

"This one will look exactly the same. No one will know which one you're using. More than likely, your Mac is being monitored by someone."

"Oh my God. You think so?"

"Father, this is a multi-billion-dollar operation. They dot all the i's and cross the t's. They don't leave anything to chance."

He didn't want to scare him, but Hamish had to add, "And, Father, they specialize in the people disappearance business."

CHAPTER 6

T HE FAMILY MEETING began with Sasha being nearly an hour late coming from practice. She was getting a ride from another parent as part of their ride share schedule. The mother apologized, telling Angie she had to stop by a store and pick up something on the way.

"We had plans, but that's okay. Maureen, I don't like it when they go places I don't know about."

"Seriously? I was just picking up something for dinner. I didn't have time before."

"Where were the girls?"

"They waited for me in the car."

Angie was livid.

"I'm asking that you not do that any longer. Just trying to be careful."

The mother was holding her tongue. Angie knew she wanted to unload some non-helpful thoughts. She prepared herself.

"You know, Angie, I've noticed Sasha has taken on a more rebellious tone lately. Not sure if you're seeing it. Probably you do. But this happens when you try to restrict them too much. Have you thought about this?"

It was so out of bounds to have this woman give her parenting advice.

"It's my right, as a parent. I don't think sitting in a car in a parking lot and me not knowing about it is safe. Too many things happen to young girls these days." She didn't want to divulge anything more, hoping this would help the woman come to her senses.

"Well, we don't have that problem in our house. We try to remain on friendly terms with our kids. That way, we don't hit as much resistance. We show them how much we trust them. Surely you trust, Sasha?"

Angie's anger was boiling. She felt Maureen was looking down on her and their entire family, not just Sasha.

"I do. I don't trust the perverts out there. They don't play by the rules, do they, Maureen?"

She left in a huff. Then Sasha stormed upstairs while everyone else was seated calmly in the living room. Angie knew she'd be working out a new schedule without the help of Maureen's transportation services.

She got Sasha to come down instead of taking her shower, which was normal. She tossed herself in the corner of the couch, grabbed a pillow, held it to her chest, and pouted.

Hamish started by explaining some facts about child sexual abuse, where predators came from, and what the new statistics were as far as abduction of teenagers and younger children. Then, to underscore his brief talk, he laid down on the coffee table in front of them five graphic pictures of dead children, four girls and one boy about Ian's age.

The boys were visibly upset, objecting strongly to the photos. Angie hoped Hamish was prepared to tackle their concerns. He let them stew.

Cora began to cry. Angie could tell her heart ached. It also showed she had a good deal of fear about what the future held.

But Sasha stared down at the photographs, without a sound and without an expression. Except that she couldn't take her eyes off the mutilated bodies.

He explained what the new rules were going to be around the house. Their schedules and who they hung around with were going to be further scrutinized. Resistance was futile, in other words. He explained the photographs that Sasha had received but did not have the phone to show them and asked their help in reporting anything out of the norm to either he or Angie.

He told them he'd die protecting them, if it took

that. But he wanted their help.

"I can't be everywhere at all times, guys. I want to be. If I could, I would. But you're going to have to meet me halfway. You're going to have to be in touch with each other, check in with us more, never leave yourself alone with a parent or kids we don't know, and certainly don't be around strange adults.

"I don't want the last photograph I have of one of you to look like one of these," he finally ended, holding up a photo of little Sylvia, only ten years old, trafficked for sex and left for dead after a snuff film.

After they were all dismissed, he turned to Angie.

"Well, how did I do?"

"You're kidding, right?" she said.

He shrugged. "I wanted to be direct."

"Oh, you were that, Hamish. But next time we have this little talk, I'm going to do it."

TWO DAYS LATER, Angie busied herself, preparing the dinner for Danny Begay and his family. Most of what she served came from their garden, except for the steaks that Hamish insisted on grilling with his secret personal recipe. She added hot dogs for the kids.

She'd picked fresh flowers for the table and had made two pies, one a chocolate cream pie that was a favorite of her family's and a wild blackberry pie, Hamish's favorite, made with fruits they picked at one of the parks nearby growing along the fence.

Just before Danny and Luci and the family arrived, her four kids were warned about their best behavior.

"We're going to have a four-year-old here, so he can't go outside around the pool area without his mother or be left alone anywhere in the house."

"Can we take him to our room?" asked Ian.

"Yes, but make sure your delicate things, like your models, Ian, are protected. He's not your age, so he's not going to want to play with things you have. He might not even know about them. Legos and Lincoln Logs might be a good fit. Or he might prefer to stay close to his parents. Sometimes little ones are like that," she stressed.

"How old are the other two?" asked Sasha.

"Ali is around nine or ten. And Griffin is six."

The girls wrinkled their noses. They'd gotten dressed up, both beginning to experiment with makeup. Apparently, it was all for naught. Angie was amused.

"You might find Ali quite interesting. He speaks several languages. Danny adopted him in Iraq when he was orphaned. I understand he's quite an active kid."

Ian and Andrew shrugged, accepting the challenge. Angie said her prayers and then opened the door to let the Begay family enter.

She was struck with how sleek and statuesque Luci

was, her beautiful dark hair hanging down to nearly her waist. Danny was not as large as Hamish, though fit and extremely handsome.

Luci handed her a dish. "I've made some southwest corn on the cob. It's a little spicey, but my kids eat it. Danny's favorite."

"Thank you." Angie took the crockery tray with the ears wrapped in foil. "Should I keep these warm?"

"If you like, yes. But you can also set them on the barbeque for about five minutes as well. Keep the foil on, of course." She pulled a covered bowl from her large bag. "Here's some Mexican cheese to drizzle on the top. I wasn't sure if anyone was allergic."

"Oh, we love cheese. This is mild, right?"

"Yes, think of it as sour cream, really. Enhances the flavor."

"Thank you. How thoughtful. Oh, I can't wait to try it."

The kids had already introduced themselves. The Begay children insisted on shaking hands. Angie noted they were formal, each of them thanking their family for hosting them. Little Ali, with his dark hair and dark eyes, looked like one of Danny and Luci's own. He also appeared to have more of a keen interest in the girls than Andrew and Ian, much to their disgust.

Danny was already outside with Hamish, inspecting his garden and the barbeque setup. At her back, she heard the subject of the pool come up. She looked at Luci.

"I'm not sure if Chester can swim, or the other two, for that matter. I told my kids not to allow him in the backyard."

"He's not a strong swimmer yet but loves the water. I think maybe next time I'll bring a life vest, if we plan to swim."

"I have one," said Angie. "I have all sizes. Required if you have a pool down here with all the kids that visit."

"Thanks very much, but I think next time. I'll walk him outside so he can see it." She turned to Ali and Griffin. "No swimming. Not today, but you can go outside."

"Mama! Mama!" Chester jumped up and down, extending his hands to her face. "I want to go."

"Yes, I'll take you. Give me your hand." She rolled her eyes at Angie and took Chester, who was going to also be big like Griffin, outside to catch up with the other children who had torn out the back door.

"How do you manage with your four now, all teenagers?" she asked as she and Angie walked together, Chester between them.

"I've got one driver and one with a learner's permit. That helps a lot, believe me. I was going to say the same for you. I can't imagine having young children again.

That was so much work. I almost feel like this is the easy part."

"Ali's been a great help. He kind of absorbs and directs the testosterone in the house when Danny is away. Griffin looks up to him so much. It's often two against one."

Chester's angelic face was all smiles as they came upon the pool. His eyes got wide.

"Next time, Chester," Luci reminded him.

Angie directed them to sit while the other kids were running back and forth on the lawn doing a game of tag.

"They seem to be occupied already, although we're going to have sweaty kids at the dinner table," laughed Angie. "Ian tries to hide it, but his voice is changing and, man, does he sport the body odor. He's like his dad in that respect."

"I noticed his red, white, and blue braces. I can see he's been raised right," remarked Luci.

"I can't claim any of that. He chose it. I think he was trying to impress his dad, truth be told. Andrew makes fun of him because he never needed braces. But Ian got all the hairy, awkward genes in the family. Hamish says it's painful to look at him sometimes. I guess that part of his growing up wasn't so pleasant."

"Danny's the same. When Ali came to live with us, Griffin wasn't nearly as athletic, and he was years younger. Ali had survived so much in Iraq, and Danny taught him how to build and use a sling-shot. For the first year after he came, Griffin had bruises all over his forehead as Ali took aim at him with packets of jam and sugar, even spoiled fruit. It was a real problem. Now to look at them, well, they gang up on Chester, poor fellow. I hope he grows taller than the both of them to get even."

"It happens."

Angie excused herself to get the rest of the dinner together. Hamish indicated the meat was almost done. He ordered the kids to come inside and wash their hands.

As she worked in the kitchen, Sasha slipped past her, running. Her makeup was smeared, her hair no longer in that perfect coif. She was barefoot, carrying her sandals over her shoulder like a movie star. An action movie star, she thought.

"Slow down there. You having fun?"

"Yes," she said with a grin. "Ali is so cool. I know how to say 'fuck you' in Arabic."

"Sasha! That's not nice."

"He asked me what I wanted to learn to say. It was my choice, Mom, not his."

"You know we don't talk like that in this house, and it is even more egregious that you have guests and you're encouraging it."

She wasn't buying any of it. Her stubborn streak was a mini version of Hamish's. Angie wondered where all this rebelliousness was coming from. She grabbed her daughter by the elbow before she could escape.

"Not here. Never here. You stop acting this way, Sasha. This is not appropriate. What do you think he thinks about you as a young lady when you ask him to translate those things?"

"We're just playing, Mom. Don't have a heart attack."

Angie pulled her back into the kitchen and drilled her a look. "I said stop it. This is not what we do. You're not using your head. It's inappropriate and not the right way to welcome new friends into our home. You don't hear your dad or I doing that, do you?"

Sasha shriveled a bit. She tried to shrug but appeared to change her mind at the last minute.

"Come on, answer me."

"No, Mom. But you guys do text dirty messages." She kept her eyes on her mother's and then gave a late smile. It wasn't a challenge but an honest look. Then she added, "Sorry, you walked right into that one."

"That's different. He's my husband. This boy is from a different family, and a brother's family at that, a brother in arms. We don't treat each other's children with that lack of respect. Should I have your dad explain it to you?"

"No, I get it. Now, can I go?"

Angie was still unsettled with Sasha's attitude but let her go anyhow. Sometimes it was just better to not pry too much, and hope for, look for the next opportunity to discuss it with her. She was learning she had to pick her battles carefully. The teens were tricky with the girls. But Sasha was acting out a lot more than Cora ever did. She hoped she wasn't missing something.

Everyone sat down to the table. Hamish led the grace they sang, holding hands. It was a relic of his grandmother's. The tune didn't rhyme because it originally came from a relative from Denmark, but that didn't matter. It was a family tradition, and the Begay kids sat quietly and watched her kids sing.

The steaks were placed on a huge platter and cut into several smaller pieces, but leaving a couple of huge ones for whomever was most hungry. That always included Hamish. Angie noted that still, at fifty years of age, he could still eat more than four grown men at any time. He'd once eaten a dozen baked potatoes just to show her he could.

The seasoned corn Luci made was fabulous, and she was promised the recipe. They didn't have room to grow their own but often got fresh corn from the Saturday farmers market.

"You interested in doing something after the

Teams, Danny? I know Harper's always talking about you," Hamish casually mentioned while wiping his moustache of barbeque sauce.

"So that's how I got the invite over to your place."

"We make people earn it. Or hadn't you heard?" Angie added.

"Oh, I get it now. I was told the admiral asked for me. Now, that impressed me," answered Danny.

"Actually, it was a bit of both. Can't talk too much about it right now because of the kids—"

"Dad, we want to hear it," interrupted Ian. "We love that gory stuff."

Danny laughed and looked at his three boys. "You three, don't say a word." He pointed with his fork.

Ali rolled his eyes. Chester looked puzzled, but Griffin smiled lovingly back at his dad. "Yes, sir."

"Dad has the best stories." Ian was still lobbying for some juicy Special Ops stories.

"What they never knew, until now, is that I make it all up. None of my stories are true," said Hamish. He looked over at Angie and winked. "Your mother doesn't much like to hear it."

"Hear, hear, a woman with impeccable taste!" said Luci. "I completely agree. At least, not at the dinner table."

Sasha and Cora were being quiet, but there was some serious staring going on between Ali and Sasha.

She'd redone her makeup and twisted her hair up on her head, looking rather pretty again.

Luci was curious about the girls. "You guys are, what, in high school? Cora, you must be a senior, right?"

"Yes, ma'am."

"How about you, Sasha?"

"I'm a freshman."

"Your mom was telling me you both play volleyball?"

They both nodded their heads.

"I always wanted to learn to play. Just never had the time," said Danny. "Probably why I've never been asked to be on any of the SEAL Teams."

"It's fun. I'll bet you could outjump me," said Hamish. "It helps to play front row when you're my height. But I used to get yelled at for not jumping high enough. My coach once called me a tree trunk."

Angie almost choked on her wine, remembering the story. "His coach threatened to send him to ballet classes if he didn't start moving more. But you should see him play Rugby."

"Ballet is for sissies," suddenly Chester said with gusto, the "s" sounds whistling between his two missing upper teeth.

Luci lightly reprimanded him, but everyone laughed. Cora spit out her soda.

"That's right, Chester. Don't you forget it either. We need men to be men and not ballerinas." Angie was going to object to Hamish's encouragement, but Luci did it for her.

"Now, Hamish, there are some very graceful and talented male ballet dancers, and I, for one, love to watch them. They have to be so athletic and flexible. All that training. But it's not for everyone, obviously."

"I can't wait until he gets in school. You're going to get those notes," Hamish said, pointing at Danny.

Danny nodded then addressed Chester. "We've seen male dancers at the Dine Games, right, Chester? The beautiful costumes? You liked watching those dancers, didn't you?"

"No. They aren't sissies," Chester said definitively. And that was the end of that subject.

"Rugby. Now that's a sport I can totally own. I'm teaching the boys."

"Never could follow the rules much," said Danny. "You ever watch those Black Haka players from New Zealand? Those guys are amazing. You ever meet Jason Kealoha from Team 3, Hamish? Pacific Islander, big guy with tons of tats? He knew some and used to play with a couple of them recreationally."

Hamish agreed. "They're wicked. I love that YouTube video where they take on the Brit team, who looked like a bunch of boarding school emaciated high schoolers in comparison."

"If you ever meet him, make Jason do the chant. It's hilarious," said Danny.

"I'd love to see that. Dad, can we meet him and have him show us?" asked Ian.

"We'll see if I can set that up. Might need your help on that, Danny."

"Happy to introduce you. You boys would love it. Not so sure Angie would like you practicing in the house, though."

"I'll second that."

The banter went back and forth until just about every scrap of food was gone. The girls helped her clear the table after refusing Luci's help. Angie laid out the pies and began to cut them, letting the girls deliver to the diners who wanted them. As she thought, the chocolate pie was a hit with the kids, especially Danny's three.

The kids went upstairs, but Chester returned when something happened and he fell. He came down crying and sat in his mother's lap. They could hear the men discussing history of human trafficking in the Navajo lands.

"You know, if he needs any help and Danny's not available, I still have lots of contacts there, even though we sold our house there years back. We both still have family there. I used to be on the Tribal Council back when I taught. Danny's mother is Miwok, but I'm one hundred percent Dine. He wasn't eligible to serve."

"Really? Good to know. Didn't know that's how it worked," answered Angie.

"Like anything, we have good chairmen and women, and we have bad ones. Not everyone has the same set of values. It's political, very political. And there are factions. Not everyone agrees on the same issues."

"I can imagine. How long did you serve?"

"About six years. Danny's grandfather—Chester was named after him—was a World War II Code Talker."

"Yes, I'd heard. How proud he must be."

"Most of the community didn't know what they were doing, because after they came back from the war, they all were told not to talk about it. And they didn't. Took years before they received the recognition they deserved. Most of them were dead by that time."

"I'd like to learn more. I think Hamish was hoping to visit the reservation. Maybe I should tag along."

"There are some amazing museums built now, lots of archival research at University of Arizona in Tucson. Fascinating."

"I imagine you're teaching your boys about their heritage."

"We have 'Indian School' at our house. They even know some of the tongue. Ali has picked up a lot of it.

He's a whiz at languages."

"My daughter told me about that. And, Luci, she mentioned something I hesitate to bring up. I guess she asked him to tell her how to swear in Arabic."

"Really? That surprises me. I doubt he does. It's not very culturally accepted."

"Hmm. Well, that's what she told me before dinner."

"You want me to check it out?"

"Please. Let me know. I'm not making a big thing about it, but I told her it was inappropriate to ask him to do that."

"Believe me, Ali can handle himself just fine. But that surprises me he'd teach Arabic swear words. His biological father would hit him if he swore, so he said he never did. He was very close to him before he died."

"Hamish told me the story. Very touching. So he's interested in the Navajo culture too?"

"Very. Absorbs it like crazy. I think he's the smartest little kid I've ever met. Deadly shot with a sling-shot too."

The men finished their discussions and made plans to get together for a trip, doing some research. Danny didn't have a deployment for a few months, as it stood right now. They began to gather the kids, and while Danny loaded up Griffin and Chester, Luci took aside Ali and brought him over to Angie.

"Did you teach the girls swear words in Arabic?" she asked.

"No. I wouldn't do that."

Luci and Angie exchanged a puzzled look. Angie commented first.

"Sasha said you taught her—"

Ali interrupted her. "Oh, that. She thinks I did. I taught her to say 'I Love You.' But she thinks she's swearing. Don't tell her, though. Much more fun that way."

CHAPTER 7

H ARPER RECEIVED INFORMATION from their FBI source that Sasha's phone had definitely been hacked, and the phone that had been used to relay the messages was not a typical burner phone purchased locally. It was more than likely something that had been purchased in Europe, which meant there was the possibility of an international connection. But it wasn't enough information to go after them.

The FBI source told Hamish it just could've been a random troll that somehow found her pictures and figured out that she was a teen, and then they started targeting her. He doubted it was any kind of organized attack where she was specifically being stalked or being set up for trafficking. But they were definitely a threat.

He told Hamish it was good instincts on Sasha's part not to answer the texts or respond to the pictures in any way.

"That's how they nail you. Better still to delete, but

this way, it gave us something to look into. If we run across something that's similar or uses the same IP address or software, we'll recognize it and contact you back. We're creating a huge database of bad actors."

"Thanks."

Although Hamish was relieved, he knew better than to one hundred percent trust the information he received. He discussed it with Harper later when they were arranging their trip to Arizona.

"I think it's a good idea to stay skeptical. You had that conversation with the kids, Hamish?"

"I did. Angie didn't approve of the way in which I handled it, but I think I put the fear of God in them. That's what I wanted to do."

"That was necessary. With what we're doing now, you really have to make sure they're clued in."

"Done and got it." He changed the subject, "I also have been looking over this paperwork that the admiral sent. This is a really sophisticated deal we're getting into here. I recognize some of these NGOs in the report. I've read about them in the paper. They're high profile. I think I've even heard their people interviewed on TV."

"Probably started off legit at one time. Now, we don't know how much of the organizations are infected. I'm not optimistic," Harper answered. "And these are the ones they know about. Think of how many fly under the radar that never get caught."

"There are so many places we could start. It's just overwhelming. You get the priest his new computer?"

"He got it yesterday."

"How much more do you think they'll be sending us, Harper?"

"No clue. I think we've got all the background. The priest will be transmitting things starting tonight, or so I was told."

"Whose idea was it to turn the priest, or did he come forward?"

"I don't have the answer to that one yet. Doesn't really matter. The president's hand is all over this. He hates these guys."

"Bet there's a story there."

"Not something we should know about. It's his option. But again, I could be all wet. So hold onto what you can, more coming. I think the strategy will become clearer the more information we get."

"Any new cases or incidents that have happened we need to be aware of?"

"Always. They're trying to decide where the low-hanging fruit is. Who they're going to specifically target on the 'get' list. Don't worry. It will be coming and very soon too."

"So you agree to my little trip to Arizona. And can you come as well?"

"Was hoping to."

"I do think this would be helpful to go see the reservation with Danny, have him explain what he knows from growing up there. But will something be coming up that will preclude that?"

"Not that I expect. I think the trip is necessary. Couldn't hurt. That seems to be a conduit that has a strong lineage, been going on for years. I think it's a logical place to at least see how the operation works if we can find that. Danny probably knows lots of people who we could talk to. I doubt they'll talk to either of us without him being there."

"Yes, he told me that."

"We're lucky to have him as a resource. When does Team 3 deploy, do you know?"

"He said a few months. So we've got time. I told him we'd go middle of next week. How does that sound?"

"I'm good with that."

"Should I arrange transportation and schedule it, or can you get that done through the admiral?" asked Hamish.

"No I'll get him to do it. I'll come down there a day ahead."

"So how's the new baby?"

"Still pooping and crying. Getting more rest, though. She's sleeping through the nights most the time."

"Oh, boy, I remember those days. I used to love the midnight feedings, just me and the little one. Sometimes I miss them. But I do enjoy getting more sleep!"

Harper chuckled. "A rare commodity here these days. Everything revolves around the baby."

"Your security holding up after the last event?"

"So far, we're clear. Nothing unusual yet."

"Venom accept the little lady yet?"

"Oh yeah, from day one when we came home from the hospital. He follows Lydia around all the time, and the baby, well, I think Venom thinks he's the father. It's really cute to see."

"How's your dad?"

"Well, that's another story. It's just one event after another. And they told me several months ago that there was gonna be a limit to what they could handle with him. As he slips in and out of being his old self, it's hard on everybody. And we don't want him to escape, but lately, he's been trying to do that. There aren't a lot of options, but at least I have a little more money to work with to get him the best kind of care, and it's a lockdown facility. Now he's escalated to 'other rules' care, which costs a lot more. I'm lucky to have it. He has to be attended to at all times or watched by someone on the staff. He used to be able to just wander around on his own, because he was harmless.

He'd get confused, but he could play cards or read or be in a group setting playing games. But now he can't be unsupervised, and a lot of the time, he spends in his room."

"Oh, I'm sorry. Of course, he's probably healthy as a horse."

"Yep, probably gonna live a long time. So I'm adjusting to this. I just keep remembering it's not really my dad who's in there. He's gone, and it's someone else who's living there right now. But on the few days when he is lucid, it's wonderful. He seems to be moved by the sight of the baby, and he's always remembering Lydia's name when she comes by, so maybe that's the best medicine for him at this point. His doctors think so. For me, I kind of get frustrated. I'm working on that."

"I don't blame you. I would feel the same way."

"I'm glad you met Danny and made that connection. Don't stay up too late reading. Remember, we want to keep our lives balanced and not get sucked into this black hole. But it's tragic what's going on, and it's so huge it's gonna be something we can't stop. All we can do is take out a few of the players. But honestly, it's going to be tough, Hamish. I'm warning you."

"I get it. I'm in it for the long haul. Just sorry I missed the last mission, so I'm definitely in this one. You need any help deciding who else you're going to task this time?"

"I think I'm going to need just about everybody. It will probably be less tactical, but we need boots on the ground doing research, checking in on investigations underway, interviewing people, and reading police reports in all the various jurisdictions. But most important is providing security for Father Flaherty. All this, somehow, we have to do it under the radar. That's the hardest part."

"I understand. Listen, I have to go help Angie with some things, so you take care. And let me know as soon as you got something and the dates that you set up. Danny's all cleared to go by Kyle, so next week sometime should work. But let me know."

"Will do."

Hamish went upstairs to check on the kids before coming down to help Angie clean up the kitchen. Everybody was working on homework, faces washed, some showered, teeth brushed. Ever since their talk, the kids had been doing their chores and cooperating with the family plan. Things were winding down.

He whispered to the boys, "You guys all ready for the camping trip this weekend?"

He got a lukewarm response, but he shrugged it off and said good night.

With all of that appearing to be in control, he met Angie in the kitchen, coming up behind her to give her a big hug and a kiss at the back of her sweet-smelling neck.

"I just wanted to say, sweetheart, that I appreciate you. You're doing one hell of a job with the kids. I don't tell you that enough."

"Thanks." She smiled up at him, turning in his arms.

"I can't take any credit for how they're all doing, how they're turning out. And it's going so darned fast, too. Hardly enough time for me to get adjusted to the fact that they'll be leaving someday for college, or whatever."

"It is going fast. I feel the same way."

"I'm lucky you're at my side, Angie. I just wanted you to know that."

"I signed up for this. Didn't know what I was getting into, of course, but we won't dwell on that."

He found that amusing. "I'm not that bad, am I?"

"I don't give you an A for how you talk to the kids about dangerous things. But the shock value certainly got their attention."

"I know. They're actually getting their homework done early these days. I love it."

"Hope it lasts, Hamish. But I was just thinking. Actually, you're fantastic. I knew it was going to be fast-paced, interesting, sometimes dangerous, and that I was supporting a man who was going to help people, help save people. That's why you do it. You're called.

I'm here to help keep some of the pieces from flying off as we're zooming through life, that's all."

They kissed again.

"Do you know when you're going to Arizona?" she asked.

"I just got off the phone with Harper, and he's arranging it. I should know within a day or two. Probably sometime next week, though. And it won't be long. Not to worry. Nothing is going to get in the way of our camping trip."

She left their embrace and went back to rinsing dishes. "The other night when Danny's family was over here, Sasha had told me that Ali had taught her how to swear in Arabic," she said softly.

"Say what?"

"How to say 'fuck you.'"

"What the fuck?" He reconsidered his response. "Sorry. Didn't mean that. Just surprises me."

"Hold on a minute. There's more to it. It's not what you think. I mentioned it to Luci, and she cornered Ali before they left, brought him over to me so I could hear it from him directly. He told us she wanted to learn how to speak a little Arabic. When he asked her what, she came up with the idea."

"It was Sasha's idea?" he asked.

"Yes, but wait. He taught her a phrase that isn't swearing at all. It translates to 'I love you.' But she thinks she's swearing."

"I don't think I'm comfortable with her doing that. Are you, Angie?"

"No, I'm not either, but I had been worried that Ali might be a bad influence on her, and it turns out he's very adult. He knew it was wrong, and he didn't do it. I'm extremely impressed and proud of him. Sasha, on the other hand, is becoming a handful these days. And I'm sure you've seen it, Hamish. I'm just not connecting with her like I want to be."

"Yeah. It's sort of like she hit fourteen, and then all of a sudden, she started becoming a different person. Is anything going on at school or are her friends changing at all?" he asked.

"Not really, except these kids from the Catholic school are new on the volleyball team this year, so maybe there's some influence there. But she doesn't spend a lot of time with them. She's mostly just at practice. Her grades are good, she seems to be happy, but what I don't like is she has this attitude all the time like she knows it all, right?"

"Don't most teenagers do that?"

"Probably."

"And one other thing I found out today. Cora told me she's started writing a Navy guy. I guess he just shipped out to Great Lakes a couple of weeks ago."

"Who? What's his name?"

"Carl something. They got reacquainted recently, and so she's writing him now. I just wanted you to know."

"Is it serious?"

"I don't know. I mean, trying to get information from Cora is worse than Sasha. I don't think it's very serious. She's still planning to go to San Diego State, still interested in nursing, so nothing seems to be off track. Her future plans haven't changed. He's from Northern California originally, but his family moved back here about five years ago. The father is a doctor. He's got an older brother in the Navy as well. Anyway, I just wanted you to know."

"I appreciate the intel, madame spy."

"Oh, stop that."

Hamish continued loading the dishwasher and then took out the trash. He held her hand in his. "Madame, may I escort you upstairs?"

"I thought you'd never ask."

As they headed toward the stairway, Angie stopped. "Oh, I forgot to tell you one other thing."

"Is this ever going to end? When am I going to get you naked?"

She giggled. "Almost done. Promise."

"This is the last time, and then I'm going to carry you upstairs no matter how much you want to talk."

"Funny. When I was having a discussion with

Sasha a couple of days ago, she said that we text dirty things. I guess we're going to have to cool that."

"And why would we do that?"

"The kids. The kids are seeing it on our phones."

Hamish pulled her into his body, placed a long, wet kiss on her mouth, and whispered. "I think we should up the intensity a little bit on that score. But yes, I fully agree, those conversations need to stay just between the two of us."

THE TRIP TO the Four Corners region was bumped up. They were to leave the next day. Danny had to do some juggling, but Angie encouraged Hamish to go and then get back before their camping trip and the big volley-ball festival this weekend she was going to take with the girls.

Harper flew in first thing in the morning, and then all three of them took off for Phoenix. They rented a car and drove up through the beautiful red rock valleys towards Sedona and then farther north to Cameron and Tuba City, then cut across towards New Mexico, continuing east.

The beautiful red hills and towering rock monuments contrasted against the poverty housed at their base. Mile upon mile of mobile homes, fallow fields, and abandoned refrigerators and vehicles littered the land. Occasionally, there would be an outpost, general store selling wares free from Federal tax. Signs advertised legal services, jewelry sales, and "authentic" Navajo art. Once in a while, they'd find a large discount supermarket, a few small casinos, gas stations, and souvenir stands, as well as dusty local bars and cardrooms.

"The kids come here to buy booze and cigarettes cheaply," Danny said.

"Where are the schools?" asked Hamish.

"We have them, but they're spread out. Some of us used to ride our horses to school back then. We're going to see my old elementary school. We have a big new high school. They now have a beautiful clinic, a small hospital, and library. Most people who make a good living move out as soon as they can. But on a positive note, there has been a big push to teach our native language to the younger ones so it doesn't die out. You heard the story?" he asked them.

"Probably not. About the Code Talkers?" asked Harper.

"Yes. During World War II, the Japanese had been cracking the codes the Marines were using during invasions, and it resulted in a huge loss of life. The son of a missionary, not Dine, who grew up speaking the language, brought it to the attention of the invasion force commanders, and the rest is history. They were responsible for saving a lot of men during those years.

The code was impossible to crack, based on animals and objects in our culture. The word for bomber became buzzard. Fighter planes became humming-birds, and so forth. The men had to memorize about four hundred words. It was never cracked."

"I never knew that," said Hamish.

"We had a large population of young men who signed up to fight, even though they weren't given the right to vote until after they came back."

"You're kidding."

"Nope. The native tribes who fought in World War II in Utah didn't get the right to vote until the 1950s, I believe. Anyway they got these kids together, many of them lying about their age, gave them uniforms, and sent them off to war."

"Brave men," added Harper. "Your grandfather was one of them, right?"

"He was. Chester Begay. Old goat face. He's the reason I became a SEAL."

"You must be very proud," said Hamish. "A true war hero."

"He always downplayed it, unless he was mad. Then we'd hear about it. He used to tell me I was spoiled. I was."

"Just seeing this, and now knowing the history, it seems so unfair how your people have been treated," said Hamish.

Danny chuckled. "Most Americans don't know it. As a country, we have a sordid history working with Native American tribes. Most the tribes in the U.S. have treaties with the government that were broken, all the time. Over the years, only a handful have not been. I was told it was like five or six out of two or three thousand. So the community doesn't trust the government, even though the lands are placed in trust for their benefit. Working with the Tribal Council is complicated too. Hard to figure out who is running the show. Some Councils are strong; some are not. It's a patchwork over the lands."

"It's all in who you know."

"Yes, and it's a closed society. I will say that doesn't mean those choices are good ones. Just because someone is connected doesn't mean they can be trusted. Lots of shady deals going on. I think many in our community suffer from being taken advantage of over and over again by people they think have their best interests at heart, when they truly have their own. It's very sad."

"So who controls this? Do the local tribal police handle this?" Harper asked.

"It's their jurisdiction. We have judges and courts. Jails. But things here are very political. You would not believe how political they can get. We are one nation but broken into many factions, clans."

"Again, who you know."

"Exactly. It isn't our way to complain. We are sup-posed to be protected by the BIA. Like everything else, the big government programs don't get the resources in time to help the people. The big shots get paid first. The people have to wait. My grandfather used to tell me that all the time."

He drove them past the school he had attended. He'd arranged for one of his cousins, who taught a blended third grade class, to speak to them.

They walked across the dusty parking lot to an open door in the middle of a school wing of classes. A diminutive woman sat behind a desk, correcting papers. Her salt and pepper hair was parted down the middle and pulled at the back of her head in a bun.

She greeted Danny warmly, speaking to him in their native tongue.

He introduced them. "This is Emma Two Toes, my grandmother. I think she was the best teacher I ever had. Taught me to read, which was so important."

She laughed. Her lined face was leathery. But her eyes sparkled as she watched Danny bring his friends to see her.

"Emma, tell my friends here about your grand-daughter, our family."

The old woman nodded, dabbed her upper lip with a tissue, and spoke, having Danny translate.

"Flora was her name, but her Dine name was Deer Dancer. She was graceful, could leap and glide across the floor. She took to the dancing early, when she was just a toddler, and by the time she started high school, she was doing exhibition dancing for festivals, state fairs, and our ceremonies. She was the pride of our family, and she could sing as well."

Hamish knew this wasn't going to have a happy ending. He braced for what he didn't want to hear.

"They were on a girls' trip in Las Vegas, she and several other girls from the village, where they met a promoter who told them he could arrange for them to go on tour. They could travel the country, performing their native songs and dances. He showed her pictures of other performers from different tribes, dressed in finery, singing for large audiences."

Danny cleared his throat and continued. "We didn't want her to go. Her mother was very sick at the time. Flora's father had gone for work in Reno but never came back. I advised my daughter not to give her permission. I promised I'd look after her. But Flora wanted so badly to go see the big city, especially Las Vegas. She wanted to be an entertainer like the dance girls she saw."

"Three of them left together and took a bus to Las Vegas. We got letters for a while, about four or five over the span of a month. And then nothing. We inquired through our local police and never got an answer. I went to see our Congresswoman, who is Dine, and she promised to look into it, but after weeks and weeks, there was nothing."

"Have you seen her since?" Harper asked.

Danny shook his head. "Never found her. One of the other girls was found working in a brothel, hooked on drugs. She said they all had worked there, but that Flora had been sold to a very rich man, and he took her away."

Emma Two-Toes added, "Her friend thought she made it big time. We know now that's not true."

They had an interview with a Tribal Council member.

"We don't have enough to keep them here, unless they want to teach or run one of the stores, perhaps do cleaning. Some make it as artists. We are teaching language and old farming techniques, hoping we can turn some of our youth into ranchers, raising livestock. But the lure of the money and the promises to make it rich is so strong. They know exactly what to say."

Hamish asked, "What about the agencies who are supposed to help support the community? Are they any help?"

"They help the kids get out. That's all they do. They lie."

"All of them?"

"No, not all. We had one company sponsor a soccer team, supposed to be playing against other tribes in the Four Corners area. Bought beautiful uniforms, balls, nets, and flags for marking. But the boys didn't have any shoes. They have grown up playing barefoot. That wasn't allowed in the league. Most of the parents couldn't afford to buy those shoes, so they just practiced on their own and never traveled or played."

"Bet it disappointed the kids," Hamish added.

"No. Kids have fun no matter what. They had beautiful uniforms, and they washed and took care of them. It made them happy. We all liked seeing their smiling faces. There are not enough smiling children's faces here."

"Indian Health does a great job manning the clinics and hospital staffing," said Danny. "Luci has helped the school write for grants for textbooks and supplies, and it's made a difference. But without a lot of private help, because none of their grandparents could read or write, many of their parents don't as well. So not many are able to go to college."

The councilman agreed to report any disappearances or new company activities in the area, and he agreed to be a resource. "You have the illegals coming from Mexico too. They come through here. They don't stay. This isn't what they're looking for. But we see the caravans coming, and they get picked up in buses and trucks. We let them. We don't want them to stay here. There is no work for them."

After speaking to several other people, asking for stories and experiences, a pattern began to emerge in Hamish's head. It did remind him of what he saw in parts of Africa, except for the militia element not being present.

An artists' cooperative was turning out artwork sold to wholesalers, which gave an almost living wage. Their federal funding gave resources to train teachers and nurses, but only a few slots were available at one time.

And although it seemed peaceful, the beautiful red land reflecting orange on their faces, they were warned by everyone not to be caught on the reservation after nightfall.

Hamish came away moved with the images of people struggling, yet still preserving their culture and old ways. There was still a sense of hope. But the tragedy that their community was losing so much of their youthful treasure was a sadness Hamish could not shake. He was embarrassed to have fought and sacrificed for a country who didn't take care or keep their promises.

But this wasn't his fight. It was theirs.

They returned to Phoenix and then took a late flight home in the sleek black plane provided by the admiral. All three of them sat in silence.

No one said a word on the way home.

CHAPTER 8

BOTH CORA AND Sasha were excited for the huge volleyball tournament coming up, an annual event that involved more than two hundred teams from various age groups. Angie invited Marie, warning her it wouldn't be a real girl's weekend. They'd be passing out waters and making sandwiches and snacks for the girls. Angie was the team mom for Sasha's team and a helper for Cora's.

"I came with you last year, remember?" Marie said as she accepted.

"That's right. I'd forgotten. So you know what you're getting into this time. Good."

"It works out fine. Connor is in Las Vegas at a conference and won't be home until Tuesday anyway."

"This year, we have the home advantage, so there's no hotel and travel, thank goodness. Less stress too."

"Except for that darned San Diego traffic. Where is it being held?"

"Convention Center. On the waterfront. They'll have overflows at other school gyms on some days. Most of our play will be at the Convention Center, which will make it easy for me to go back and forth for both girls."

"Tell me what I can bring."

"Just your patience, Marie."

Hamish and the two boys went on a beachside camping trip, which wasn't what they'd been asking for these past months, but it was a good first step. She watched as the three amigos loaded up Hamish's truck, remembering things last minute here and there, such that when they were done, they had packed way too much gear. Hamish left it that way, and they took off. Poor Ian had barely enough room in the second seat, surrounded by camping and fishing gear. They even brought their own griddle so Hamish could make pancakes, maybe fry some fish if they caught any. The campsite they rented came with an ample supply of firewood, but Hamish being Hamish, that wasn't nearly enough, so they brought enough wood to fill an oil drum. It was way overkill. But that was the way he did everything.

She said good-bye to the happy trio and then drove over to Marie's to pick her up. Sasha and Cora were already with their teams and at the complex. One of the mothers texted her the court numbers.

Marie brought a four-inch foam pad to sit on. "If I can recall, and it was all a blur last time when we were done, my butt hurt something fierce."

"I have two folding chairs that are allowed in the gym, but they usually provide seating. Bring it just in case."

She had a large pink water cannister she carried with a strap around her neck. She strapped in, and Angie began the short drive to the Convention Center.

"What are the boys doing this weekend?" Marie asked.

"Camping. They're over at Soda Rock Beach."

"Never been there. Good weather today, not too hot."

"Hamish almost didn't have room for Ian, he packed so much. Happens every time. But they won't want for anything, for sure."

This conversation didn't segue to any part of Marie's life since she had no children. Angie was curious about that but didn't want to pry.

"Like I've said before, don't know how you do it, Angie."

"Sometimes it's exhausting. But it's a labor of love. It's everything I ever wanted in life. Would be totally different if Hamish weren't into the family thing. He didn't have a very happy childhood. I think that's why he works so hard with our four."

"I like kids. I just never wanted to be a mother," Marie suddenly said. The comment surprised Angie. "We tried for a while, but when I didn't get pregnant, we just left it at that. He would have left that decision up to me, but I didn't want to adopt. So our lifestyle is so much simpler than yours. Heck if I know why I never have enough time for things. Kind of crazy, isn't it?"

"I think we fill up the space with stuff. We fill up our days with promises and obligations. I think we all overpromise. Besides, you have your trainings and your marathons."

"Connor says we'll be spending more time in Las Vegas. One of the big companies he consults with is based there. So I guess I'll get to see some fantastic shows. He's used to coming up there with some of his buddies from the Teams. Poker tournaments. So he knows Vegas. Otherwise, it would be overwhelming."

"I'd get lost," said Angie.

"He might get them to give him an apartment there."

"Oh, good," Angie said, but it wouldn't have been anything she'd want Hamish to do. Besides, it would be nearly impossible to get him to agree to such a thing in the first place. But she kept these things to herself. "The job is working out, then. I'm glad."

"It helps to have the extra income. We're planning

some trips. Haven't taken a vacation in over three years."

"I know when Hamish was on the Teams, it was hard to schedule vacations because plans could change quickly."

"I certainly know that."

They arrived at the parking structure they were to use to the side of the complex. Angie noted the row and floor where she parked on the back of the ticket at the entrance, and they walked the breezeway over to the main hall itself.

Immediately, the sounds of hundreds of girls shouting, chanting, and cheering interspersed with whistle blowing and spectators clapping bombarded them. Once inside, all conversations would have to come to an end because the noise was so deafening.

Angie checked her phone and found Sasha's court first. She met up and introduced Marie to the other team mother who came with supplies Angie had purchased and sent along with Sasha earlier. She waved to her daughter, who ran over and gave her a hug and kiss.

"Hi, Marie!" she said. Then she focused on her mother. "Mom, they have this darling t-shirt over at the tournament store. It's pink and black and has the festival lettering all over it. Can I get one?"

"I'll go over with you when you have a break.

When do you play?"

"We're up now."

"Well, get yourself over there, silly." She watched her lanky daughter run like a giraffe to the team huddle.

Angie looked at the opposing team, who were giants compared to Sasha's team. She pointed to them. "I have a feeling we're going to get killed. They all look like Hamish's Scottish cousins."

Marie laughed and nodded. She held up her fingers, crossed.

Sasha's team won in four games, surprisingly. The girls set up a base outside in the corridors to the auditorium. She finished handing out snacks and waters to everyone and then texted and left to visit Cora's team, who was in the middle of their match. Marie went with her.

They spent the day going back and forth. Angie had to do a pharmacy run to get some bandages, sports wrap, and antibiotic cream. They had good matches and matches where the other team blew them out of the water. They had comebacks and disappointments. It was overall a good day, and both girls' teams moved up to the next bracket.

Cora was going to come over when her match was done. Sasha's team was refereeing. Then they could go home. Angie went over to the tournament shop to purchase the t-shirt Sasha wanted.

When she returned to the court, Sasha had traded with someone else for the line judging. She glanced over the group sitting with the coach and didn't see Sasha anywhere.

"Have you seen Sasha?" she asked Marie.

"I think she ran over to the lavatory."

"When was that?"

"It's been a while. This is the second game."

Angie asked several of her teammates if they knew where she was, and no one knew. Even the parents hadn't seen her leave. Her blood pressure was beginning to rise.

She ran to the bathrooms, starting on the left side and then checking the right. She called in every women's restroom she could find. She searched under locked doors when no one answered. There was no sign of her anywhere.

Now she was beginning to get nervous. She confronted the coach.

"What do I do? Should I get them to make an announcement, ask her to call me?"

"She has her phone?" asked Lori, the coach.

"Yes. She has a new one. Where are her things, do you know?"

"Her bag's right over there."

Angie unzipped the bag, rummaging for anything

she could, and didn't find the phone. She walked to the announcer booth and asked for them to make a request Sasha contact her team, gave the court number.

Hearing her daughter's name over the loud speaker sent a chill down her spine. But the twenty minutes afterward was even worse. There was no return call, no message, no sighting.

She and Marie checked the bathrooms again. They asked about private restrooms and were ushered upstairs to the convention center's business offices.

"I don't think he's here today, but we have the whole place under video surveillance. What court was she?"

"Court 28, right over there."

"And how long since someone's seen her?"

"Since about forty-five minutes ago, maybe longer."

They watched the video of Sasha asking a team-mate to take her place in the corner, giving her the red lines flag. Sasha jogged to the restroom on the right, the bigger one. And then that was all. No more Sasha. She disappeared after she went to the restroom.

Angie still scanned the crowds, hoping to see her face. She caught Cora on her way over to court 28.

"Mom. Have you found Sasha?"

"Not yet. Did she come over to your court?"

"No. Mom, you're scaring me. She has to be with someone."

"I've asked. You heard the announcement."

Cora's face was shriveled, embroiled in heavy worry. Angie figured hers looked the same way. She didn't want to panic, but the longer time went on, the harder it was to stay calm.

She closed her eyes, willing her daughter to appear, but when she opened them, there was the same noise, the same milling around of several hundred people, whistles blowing and cheers going up.

But there was no Sasha. She needed to get the police involved and right away. And then she'd have to make that call to Hamish.

CHAPTER 9

HAMISH RACED FROM the campsite back to their home in San Diego after receiving the call from Angie. There were so many things going through his mind. His heart, of course, was hurting, his blood pressure spiking, almost leaving him breathless. He knew he had to calm down and be careful.

And especially since they'd learned all of this new information about the trafficking business, it made all the possible tragic outcomes flash through his brain, making everything worse. He knew how bad it could be. Try as he could, he couldn't shake the horrible feeling in his stomach that this was so far out of his control there was no clearcut solution. The pressure was making him feel confused.

He knew this was sort of a fog of war type of thing. Something warriors found when they discovered themselves in an untenable situation or something so dangerous that it was likely there were going to be multiple sacrifices made. The only question was when would be his turn.

His phone started blowing up while he was driving. The two boys sat stoically in the second seat, Andrew electing to sit next to Ian who was in tears ever since he'd heard about Sasha's disappearance. He loved that about Andrew, the fact that he could focus in on what he could do instead of what he couldn't do.

Right now, Hamish was trying to find that balance and that concentration. But the incessant phone calls and text messages received were making it hard to keep that focus. He even got a phone call from the President of the United States, extolling his concerns and offering to give whatever assistance he could to Harper and Hamish and the team. He asked him if there was anything in particular he could use.

Hamish told him, "Prayers. And maybe more special agents, people you trust." He explained the scenario, the fact that this had occurred at the convention center with thousands of undcragc girls and too few chaperones to control them all, the doors wide open to the general public to come and go with no checks. It was not a controlled scenario or one that the team would be able to easily limit. Impossible was the word he was thinking of.

"There are just too many people, too many children, and too much to investigate in the middle of the chaos of the festival. I feel so helpless," he told the president.

"I do understand. Rest assured, they're going to come up with something. Maybe cancelling the festival would help with some of that."

"Sir, at this point, I don't know. I just know that it's gonna be difficult to get the kind of information we need to even start looking for her."

"I'm sending a couple of my best, men I would use to protect my own family if it ever came to that. They're both special Federal agents. They've been with me ever since I was a senator. Think they can help. They'll be looking for you and calling you direct."

He gave Hamish the names, but Hamish wasn't going to remember them.

Harper was on his way down from Sonoma County. He had directed two former teammates to protect Lydia and the baby and look in on their neighbor. He promised he'd be showing up at the convention center, which was where everyone was gathering, probably by the time Hamish got there.

He looked in the rearview mirror at Ian's face as he continued to tear down the freeway.

"You guys are real troopers, both of you. I'm so proud of you. We'll make up for this trip, I promise. What you need to know is your dad is lucky enough to be working with some of the best people out there. If anybody can find her, this group of people will. And I promise you, I will not rest until we do. We *will* find her."

Ian didn't want to look him in the eyes, probably because he was so distraught and so filled with tears. He stared out the window at the passing scenery but nodded his head glumly.

Andrew tapped Hamish on the shoulder. "Dad, we know you're doing your best. This isn't your fault at all. It's what you talked about the other night. I think that's what makes it worse for us, because now we know what can happen. But—"

Andrew's lower lip quivered as he broke, unable to continue. The duplicate reaction from Ian forced long hot tears to flush his own cheeks, dripping on his T-shirt. His nose ran, and he let it continue to just drip.

They dropped all their gear in the garage at the house, and he instructed the boys to go upstairs and pack a bag for three or four days with clothing and to bring all their school books. He had arranged for Neil Gorsey's family, another former teammate on SEAL Team 5 to take the boys, as the family had two sons at similar ages. And they were friends.

He called Harper to let him know about the president's message but only got voicemail, so he left a message.

They were going to have to find a place for Cora to

stay, but he hoped Angie was working on that.

THEY'D BEEN OFFERED the large conference room upstairs overlooking the main floor of the convention hall, Harper had told him, with a bird's eye view of all the courts. He couldn't fathom how they were going to continue the afternoon pool of games, and of course, it was supposed to go on all day tomorrow, as well. But that was the least of his problems right now.

It was just a complete nightmare to even think of managing the information, with the flow of people back-and-forth. It was going to be impossible.

Other text messages came in from other Team guys asking if they could help. He sat down while waiting for the boys and answered several of them. A handful mentioned that they'd come by the center and see if they could lend assistance. Even though it had been over a year since he'd last been to a Team 5 function after his detachment, once brothers, always brothers. He would do the same for any of them.

Several years ago, a member of Team 5 had gone into the police force after detaching, and his daughter was kidnapped and murdered. The whole team got involved in her search and rescue and helped the police weed out the perpetrators. Unfortunately, for her, she had been found too late.

Don't go there, Hamish. It's not going to end this

way.

He knew that time was of the essence. The faster they could get the information they needed, the more manpower they could devote to it, the better chances of her being able to be returned unharmed. He doubted it was going to be a ransom situation. And he desperately hoped they were amateurs rather than a well-oiled cartel group.

He dropped Andrew and Ian off at the Gorsey family's house, gave them both a hug, and watched them be greeted by good friends. It was the perfect place for them for now, Hamish thought. Neil, his former Teammate, came up and embraced him, giving him a slap on the back.

"Hanging in there?"

Hamish looked at him, his eyes still filled with tears. "What do you think, Neil? I'll get through it, you know I will. There's only one outcome I'm focused on. And I'm gonna fucking fight to get that."

"You do that. You fight. And you let us help you. Don't be turning down help, okay? Don't take it all on yourself. We're the brotherhood. We're there for you and will do anything for you, Hamish. Swear to God. And there are a hundred guys behind me, trust me on that."

"Thanks, man."

"Text me or let me know if you've got any news. I'll

promise to pass it around. If you're looking for some-body, if there are people in the area that are suspicious or suspect, and you want to release any of that infor-mation, we're not on deployment, and we got manpower here. We would do almost anything for you. You need somebody to bust down some doors or pull some cars over? You know we'd be there, Hamish. These guys won't get away if they're still here."

"Yeah, I'm hoping they weren't prepared for the kind of pressure we're gonna give them. I'm really hoping they didn't think this out well enough. I hope they panic, and I hope they just return her. There's no way in hell they're going to get away with it."

"That's right. You just remember that, okay? And don't lose faith man. You have to think clear, and you have to remember all the stuff you have to check out and do. There's a lot. But you need to share any of that? Don't you dare hesitate."

"I won't. Thanks for the talk. Take care of my boys."

"Like they were my own, Hammy."

His eyes were still watering as he drove the freeway, turning off at the harbor, the large convention complex coming into view. There was a line of about thirty cars to enter the parking structure, which pissed him off. He came to a uniformed officer who was directing traffic and rolled down his window.

"I'm the father of a girl who has gone missing from this event—Sasha McDougall. Is there someplace where I can park where I won't be towed?"

"Sir, I can't authorize that. I'm sorry." She was young, probably hadn't received the information yet. So Hamish didn't want to push her.

"It's just that I'm so out of time. I need to find my daughter, please," he said as the tears began to roll down his cheeks again.

Staring behind him at the line of cars he was holding up, she put her hand out to them and directed him to turn toward the front of the complex. At the end of the parking lot was a red fire and rescue truck as well.

"You go up there and tell him I said it was urgent. Explain to them the situation and see if they'll let you. If they won't, come back here, and I'll push you through the line. Best of luck, sir."

"Thanks, ma'am."

He sped to the entrance and, after speaking to a uniformed officer there, was directed to a police designated parking spot.

He'd brought his computer, and with it strapped over his shoulder, he ran inside the convention center. The crush of people and the deafening sounds of whistles and cheers and even laughter, as teams of girls and chaperones walked past him, lugging gear, knee pads down around their ankles stunned him. It was the

crush of everyday life, people participating in a sport-
ing event and having fun, talking about ordinary things
young girls talked about. All the while, his Sasha was
gone, and the whole world didn't wait for her return.

It was painful for Hamish to see the stark contrasts
to this.

But when he entered the convention hall, the sound
was ten times worse, drowning out any attempt at
conversation, a confusion of parents, officials, teams,
and coaches. Groups of college coaches on recruiting
trips lined several of the courts. There must have been
over three thousand girls, at least. It was a completely
uncontrollable environment—no place for a kidnap-
ping investigation. His chances were doomed.

He walked toward a group of uniforms who had
gathered behind a table.

"I'm Hamish McDougall. I'm Sasha's father. I'm
looking for my wife, Angie, and I'm looking for
perhaps people who are part of a task force that's been
formed?"

One of the officers stood and took him over to a
stairway. "They've set up a command center upstairs,"
she shouted.

Hamish could barely hear her.

"I believe your wife is there now."

"Thanks." He began climbing the stairs when she
stopped him.

"Wait a minute. I gotta ask you first. Are you carrying any weapons?"

"What the fuck?"

"No need to swear at me, sir. I'm just doing my job. The executive offices require everyone upstairs be unarmed."

"Are you fuckin kidding me? Did you check all these parents? There must be some hundred or more people carrying. Did anyone check their bags or make them go through a metal detector. The place is fuckin wide open, ma'am."

"It's the rules of the upstairs office."

"You mean they leave all these kids without anyone defending them except their parents, and you're worried about some executive staff? One of these kids has been kidnapped for Chrissakes. And yes, I fuckin' am carrying. I always do, and I know how to shoot better than you do, I'll guarantee you of that!"

He'd landed his point. She relented without saying a word.

He was still swearing about it as he climbed the stairs, mumbling, "No metal detectors, no bag checks. They're lucky nothing has happened yet. This could be a mass casualty right here affecting our best and brightest, our most vulnerable population."

He noted to himself, if it were up to him, everyone should be required to carry a firearm. Then maybe people would think twice before coming for their treasure.

"A room full of sitting ducks!"

The conference room, compared to the large hall, was relatively quiet. Angie was seated on a side chair over against the wall with Cora at one side and Marie on her other side. Tables were being erected, and computers brought in as a dozen or so agents and officers were setting up a command center. Hamish recognized the equipment, but he didn't recognize Harper or any of the men working the task force spread. His first commitment was to Angie.

She was looking down in her lap. Clearly, she was exhausted.

"Dad! I'm so glad you're here!" said Cora, who had been the first one to notice him as she ran to his arms. Angie looked up and finally smiled. She too wrapped her arms around him, melting into his embrace.

"Sweetheart, I'm so sorry about all this. I swear we're gonna do everything we can—"

"Oh, shut up, Hamish, and just hold me for a few moments please." Then he felt her begin to shake then sob. She'd been holding out, and now the flood of emotions was erupting. "Our baby, our baby is gone. I feel so helpless. I just feel so out of my element."

Hearing her little voice, wobbly and unsure, broke his heart. He dared not show her his pain. It would not help their situation. It would only add panic to her already caving insides.

"Of course you do. That's why it was designed this way. These guys know this. Come on, you've got to be strong. We're gonna do this. We're gonna get her back."

"I hope so." He could see she was close to collapsing. Her eyes were soft, resigned to bad news, filled with tears. "This is hell, Hamish. I'm just so sorry for what happened."

He glanced over Angie's shoulder at Marie. He didn't feel the warmth back toward her since hearing the information Angie had shared about Connor. After their embrace ended, he thanked her for coming.

"Thanks for being here, Marie. I think after they're done questioning you can probably leave. I think Angie and I are going to have to make some tough decisions here. But thank you for being here with Angie."

"No problem. I'm so sorry, Hamish. Truly. Let me know if there is anything we can do for your family."

"Let me just check in with the team first. But thanks."

He went over to the task force and began introducing himself around until he found their liaison captain, Rodney Carson, one of two of the special agents that were promised.

"Nice to meet you, Rodney. Is Harper here?" he

asked.

"Not yet. Listen, Hamish, we're setting up. In about five minutes, I'm going to give you a briefing, okay? And you tell me what kind of assets you have coming?"

"Happy to. Um, just a quick question. Has anyone interviewed Angie's friend, Marie, over there?"

Rodney looked her over. "No, don't think she got a sit down. You want us to?"

"I'd like to send her home, but I'd like her interviewed first. Do you mind getting someone on it?"

"Sure thing. Anything specific you are looking for?"

"Ask her what her husband does."

"Will do." He called a uniformed woman over and gave her a clipboard. She crossed the room and took Marie aside. They sat at a table, Marie's back to the rest of the room.

"I'll let you work. Call me when you're ready."

"Roger that. Hey, nice to meet you. Wish it was under better circumstances. The president says nice things about you."

"Hope so," answered Hamish.

He returned to Angie. "What have you found out?"

"Not a whole lot. They're trying to find surveillance footage from somewhere. Just asked me a lot of questions about Sasha, if she'd ever run away, that sort of thing. I think they aren't letting the team go home until they talk to everyone, even the parents and coaches."

"Did any of them see anything?"

"No, that's the thing. She asked to use the restroom and left on her own. I would have asked her to take someone with her, but I was buying a t-shirt. She went alone."

"Did she ask Marie permission?"

"Marie? Heck no. She was watching the game. They were refereeing. She was watching the other game." She pulled herself away, bending backward, and gave him a frown. "What's going on?"

"Just a vibe I'm getting."

"She's my friend. I trust her."

"I'm sorry. I've got conspiracy theories on the brain. I'm grasping at straws."

"Well, grasp somewhere else. She's golden. I vouch for her. But do what you will."

Hamish knew she was irritated with him a tad. Just then, Rodney called him over to the tables.

"Okay, Hamish, I've got another ten agents on their way from the San Diego office. My understanding is that you have a few as well. Several have wandered into the hall already, looking all beefy and tatted up. After living in San Diego all this time, I can sure spot a Navy SEAL when I see one. They don't tend to blend in too well."

It was the lightest moment of the day so far. But Rodney was right.

"I'll deal with them. Nobody's going to interfere with your investigation. This isn't what we do. We're the action figures. We gather intel, and then we act. Emphasis on the act. Give me a manual and charts, and I'm toast. I'd never lead a team."

"I think you underestimate your skills. But no worries. You're solid. Anyone you bring in will be given carte blanche. I'll include them in the briefings." He hesitated. "So what's this about the girlfriend?"

"Her husband worked with Harper on the Teams, but now works as a consultant. First, I don't see many former SEALs being desk consultants, advising companies what to do on policy or political on things. But I could be wrong."

"We'll get it checked out. Trust me."

"So you can count on at least another ten from our side. Harper should be here any minute, and he'll let you know who. What are you piecing together here?"

Rodney pointed to a pair of men reviewing surveillance tapes in the corner. "We're in the process of trying to identify who went into the bathroom. We think she was abducted there."

"You need help with that, because my guys could do that for you."

"Sure. We've got one tape reader, though. I'll see if they can find another."

"How do you handle the scene like this? All these

people in and out. All these young girls? Are they going to continue with the festival?"

"Two quick answers," said Rodney. "We don't, and we aren't sure. We don't have jurisdiction to close it down, since we don't have it verified that a crime has been committed. We think it has, and we're about to issue an Amber Alert, which is gonna make everything go crazy in a hurry. But if we can just verify that there was an abduction, that gives us a lot more clout. We can maybe lean on them. But even more important, if we can place her getting into a vehicle, we might have a chance to catch a license plate, and that helps with the alert. Always better when you have the car identified."

"Got you."

"But I've talked to the festival promoters, and they aren't budging. They want to go forward with it. I guess teams have come from all over the United States, some girls looking to meet up with college recruiters for scholarships and such. So they don't want to send them home. And there's no indication that other girls are at risk. But the truth is, they didn't plan for this contingency. It will affect everything they do from now on is my guess. They should have thought about it before. But the world isn't the same place as it once was, is it?"

"No, sure isn't."

"It's impossible to predict all this stuff. They were smart, though, I think these guys who took her planned it all out. That probably has me worried the most."

"So you think she was targeted."

"If I had to guess, and you don't want to hear this as the father of that beautiful little lady, I'd say yes she was indeed targeted. But have faith. We're smarter than they are. And we have more resources. They also don't know the President of the United States is an ally."

"Or could that be part of the reason?"

"I don't think so. They'd be pretty fuckin dumb to try to pull that off. No, some of what you and your Team does could be coming up on someone's radar and they could be looking to make a statement. I think you might be the target, Hamish. And what's worse than to put your daughter in danger? Nothing worse than that."

He wished he hadn't asked so many questions. All the rest of the description Rodney gave him went in one ear and out the other. The possibility that he might have caused this in some way kept ruminating around in his head. He was about ready to scream.

Just then, Hamish got a tap on the back. He turned.

Harper stood there with his arms outstretched. He grabbed Hamish and squeezed him tight. At the last minute, he whispered in his ear, "Whoever did this, their life is going to end very soon. I promise you that, my friend."

CHAPTER 10

RODNEY FINISHED THE interview with Angie. Marie had been done several minutes before, working with another team of agents. Cora was sitting by herself, very much looking like a fifth wheel. Angie could tell she didn't care for sitting around listening to everybody work. She was concerned about her sister, Angie knew that, but it was making her nervous the longer she stayed with them. No doubt, she was also hearing tidbits of information that upset her as well.

Angie approached Hamish and the team.

"Hamish, I'm thinking I should find somebody on Cora's team to take her back home with them. Or I could take her home with me, although I'd like to stay if I can be of use. What do you think?"

"Either one is fine with us here." He turned to the team and got nods all around. "Do what you feel's best."

"Are you sure it's safe at home? I guess I should

also ask, should I be driving around without a guard? Does it look like that would be necessary?"

"I don't think so, Angie. We're not coming across anything like that. No, you go home just in case she shows up there or somebody else comes to the door. I've got two of my guys there, and you'll be more than safe. They won't let anyone interfere, and they'll be watching the whole street."

"Okay then. I'll take her home with me. I think she'd like that."

They kissed.

"I'm going to strangle you if you don't keep me updated," she added.

"So noted. You'll get an Amber Alert when we're able to send one. We're close."

"Which is a good sign, right?"

"Means we're identifying someone as a suspect."

"Can I see the film?"

Hamish looked to get reassurance from Rodney and the others. They stepped aside and let Angie look at the video of the bathroom. Sasha washed her hands and then two men came in and gagged her. There was a struggle as she tried to free herself, but then she lost the fight, as if she'd been drugged. She was wobbly but able to walk through the doorway and down the great hall, both men holding her up. Parents watched as they passed by teams of girls and chaperones, unaware she was being abducted. No security guards were present anywhere.

Angie's heart sank. It was hard to watch, the evidence blatantly in front of her. Sasha had been kidnapped.

"That's it. We have another tape of her getting into a car, which we'll file on the Amber. It's a lead. But it also proves she's in danger, sweetheart."

His loving arm slung around her shoulder as she silently wept. She didn't know where she was getting the tears from, since she'd been crying non-stop for the past nearly three hours.

Like a zombie, she approached Marie and Cora. "Okay, let's go downstairs. Grab your bags, and I'm gonna take you and Marie home. Let's check in with your coach first, okay?"

The three of them marched down the stairs. First, Angie checked with Sasha's team. One by one, the parents had been interviewed along with their daughters, and they were nearly done. Coach was annoyed, but under the circumstances, it was tolerated.

"Are we still on for tomorrow then? Have they closed the festival?"

"I doubt they will, Angie. I mean this is a big deal, their big fundraiser, and you know some of these teams have been saving all year to come here. I don't think they will. Are you going to be okay with getting Cora back here tomorrow? One of us could pick her up."

"I've got lots of help, so it won't be a problem. But if anything changes or you hear about a cancellation, please let me know. I'm not in the loop on that," she answered.

"Will do."

One of the parents ran up to her, presented her with Sasha's volleyball bag.

Angie fought back the tears. She still had to check in with Cora's team. She wasn't about to lose it yet. There would be time later tonight when she could, and she knew she would.

The three of them marched over to the other team's court, where the same thing was happening with the parents and the interviews. But they were on their last one.

Cora hugged her teammates, and there were tears shed all around. The coach told Angie that, based on today's performance, they would be starting in the afternoon pool, so she'd have a chance to sleep in, and Angie was happy with that.

"You make sure and keep me informed in case they cancel this or it gets changed to a morning pool, okay?" she asked the coach.

"No problem. I doubt it'll change. And I'm so sorry. I'm really so sorry. I hope they find her soon."

"Thanks, Stan. I appreciate it. They have a great

team."

The coach looked at Cora, tapping her shoulder. "Listen, if your head's not in the game, Cora, you have my permission to stay home. Under the circumstances, everybody would understand."

Cora looked at him like he had three eyes and ten blue noses. "Are you kidding me? I want to use it to just get fired up and play my very best game. I'm not going to let this interfere. Besides, there's nothing I can do but sit around and cry about it. I mean, there's just nothing I can do. It's better than sitting upstairs with all the cops."

He chuckled. "That's my outside hitter. Killer when she wants to be. Okay, Cora you get some rest, and we'll see you tomorrow afternoon."

The three of them left the auditorium down through the grand hallway. The police had corded off one of the women's bathrooms. A full forensic team was going over everything and a small crowd had gathered around them.

Angie's phone zapped along with all the phones in the hallway, and it was the announcement from Hamish that they issued the Amber Alert.

All she wanted to do was get herself and her daughter home.

As they walk down the stairs and cross the breezeway to the parking structure, they observed several news vans parked in front of the garage. Cameramen and reporters were running up the steps, racing to try to get an exclusive interview. Apparently, now it was going to be on TV, so this would be the end of the low-profile part. The rest was going to be a zoo. It wasn't anything she was looking forward to.

Cora was completely quiet sitting up front with her. Each time Angie looked in the rearview mirror, she met Marie's eyes. Something in the way Marie looked at her triggered something, and she wasn't sure exactly what it was, but she tried to put it out of her mind. Their car slowly moved through the late afternoon traffic. Eventually, they got Marie dropped off.

Her friend tapped on the driver window. "Angie, you call me if you need anything, okay?"

"I will. Are you going to be alone then?" Angie asked her.

"Yeah, Connor doesn't get home till Tuesday."

"I'd offer my company, but I really need to be home with Cora."

"Totally understand, as you should. I wanted to mention I was getting some strange vibes upstairs. They questioned me about Connor and his job. Do you know anything about that?"

"Not a thing," Angie lied.

"I was wondering if they wanted me to keep my distance from you for some reason. Am I just being crazy, or is there something to that? They don't think Connor or I—"

"Don't be silly. Why would they think that, Marie? They're just trying to be thorough. I wouldn't worry about it. That's just investigating work. I was grilled too."

"Well, you do call me if you need anything, and I'll be home so if you need me to run Cora over to the gym in the morning, I'd be happy to do it. Honest."

"Thanks for your help today, Marie."

Cora leaned over and said goodbye to her as well.

On the way home, her daughter was slightly more talkative.

"Do you think this had anything to do with the dirty messages she was getting? Am I an idiot for thinking that, Mom?"

"Cora, I'm not sure about anything anymore. I'm tired, and I just want to go to bed. What I am learning, though, is that there are no coincidences. We're connecting dots that may not need to be connected. But once we find out the facts and that means finding out who sent those text messages, that's still on the table. Once we find out what's going on with that, we'll be able to put more together. I have a hard time thinking they're related. But if they are, they'll find it. They're really good."

"I called Carl today and told him. I hope that was

okay."

"Of course, sweetie. What did he say?"

"He wanted to bail on Great Lakes and come back to San Diego to help. He was angry, Mom. I'm going to have to be careful how much I tell him, because I feel like he's right at that edge—he could quit and ruin his career. He wants to come back and help so bad."

Angie laughed. "He sounds like your dad."

"He reminds me of him. Exactly."

"Then you're in for a treat, sweetie. Hang on to a guy like that. But I agree, don't push him over the edge.

"Carl's better off doing what he's doing at Great Lakes. But thank you for telling me."

"So where are the boys again?"

"They're at Neil and Sheila's. I wanted them to have some friends to play with, and I was concerned that I couldn't handle everybody with Hamish not here to help out. Safer for them to be over at their house. You and I have a girls' night at home all to ourselves. Should I stop and get some pizza?"

"That would be great."

She pulled up to their favorite pizza joint. Angie encouraged her to come in to the store with her.

"I'm fine. I'm just going sit here in the car."

"No, you're not. We're not doing that anymore."

"But, Mom, I'm an adult now."

"Non-negotiable. Come on."

They brought the pizza home. Angie didn't realize she was so starved. She checked with Luke and Brian, the two men who were waiting just outside their door, asking them if they wanted anything.

They had themselves all set up for a camp out. She offered them the living room couch, which was gratefully accepted. They told her they were going to take turns doing rounds of the house and sleeping. In addition, Luke said that the police were going to be doing two-hour drive-bys.

"Angie, have you ever seen anybody hanging around the house, lately? Anyone we should be looking for? Does that ever happen?" Luke asked.

"Well, it's a tourist area, so there's VRBO people, but they're so obviously different than what you're talking about. It's families with kids, and they're here for the beach, the sun, and to see all the attractions in San Diego. We don't really see people loitering around. If you'll notice, with all the flags flying here, we've got military families all over the place. Police and fire too. It would be an odd neighborhood to loiter around. That's why we bought here years ago."

"Got it."

"Around here, if you don't fly your flag, they come ask you what's wrong with you."

Both the men laughed.

She closed the memories of the horrible day by

locking the front door. After they ate, she went upstairs and took a long hot shower. She'd held up well, but now, in the privacy of her own room, she let it all come tumbling out.

She dropped to the floor and let the warm water sluice over her head and down her back, washing away all the evil, the tears, and the memories she never wanted to have.

Tomorrow would be another test.

CHAPTER 11

H ARPER RECEIVED A message Father Flaherty had uploaded a document.

"Hamish, Rodney, got an update from the priest."

He went to his computer and found the word file, clicking on it. Hamish looked over his shoulder. Rodney was on the phone and indicated he'd be right over.

The document was roughly three pages, but it listed some great resources. First, he listed the three main non-profits his charity worked with. At the top was the Indigenous People's Project, along with Freedom Train and Migrant Services, Inc. He mentioned that the Indigenous People's Project was where most of their referrals went.

He gave names of contact persons at each of these, which would give them references to investigate. He also gave names of transportation companies used to move people from different areas. Many of the individuals they were servicing came in through the Phoenix hub but were transported all over the U.S., depending on their documentation and sponsorship status.

One of the companies he listed was called Nevada Home, and the company's home office was in Las Vegas. But it also had an office in Phoenix. Bernie Isaacson was named as the GM, but a footnote mentioned that Bernie was a member of Nevada Junior Senator Mark Harris' staff.

Hamish searched his computer and found a picture of Mr. Isaacson, an affable-looking balding man with a moustache wearing a business suit. In the photo, the credits indicated he was in charge of Harris' Forward Planning Committee, also listing him as a political consultant dealing with immigration reform.

"He's a heavyweight, I'll bet," said Hamish.

Rodney approached, scanning the document. "This is great stuff. We have a lot to go on here." He faced Harper. "We'll do a careful deep dive into these entities, an untitled FBI cover probe for background sort of thing. Something that won't red flag it at the higher levels."

"Can we help with any of that?" asked Harper.

"No, I can't give you that authority. But I'll have my own guys on it, people I trust."

Harper showed his disappointment.

"Your primary concern is to help us find Sasha. That's priority one. The rest of this we'll put together, but right now, it's all about the rescue.

The priest had also made notes at the bottom about concern for his safety. He said he hadn't noticed any protection and wondered how long before he would be able to go into the Witness Protection Program.

"He's nervous, for good reason," said Rodney. "But he's nervous."

"He isn't supposed to notice the guys guarding him, is he?" asked Hamish.

"No, actually, that's a good sign. But we don't want him jumpy, bringing attention to himself. You do remember he felt like the organization was one step ahead?" added Rodney.

"I'd feel better if I could have a couple of my SEALs stay with him," said Harper. "He's a valuable asset. We're used to doing this. Got lots of practice overseas."

"If you want to, sure. When you've set it up, I'll need their I.D.s so I can inform my guys."

From across the room, one of his men shouted, "We are getting tons of tips on the Amber Alert, guys. I've got sightings from San Diego all the way up to Seattle, even one in New York."

Rodney had a team going through all the tips, prioritizing which ones to follow up on first. They were going to focus on local tips in the San Diego area.

Another of the team called out, "Okay, we got a KW on Bruno here."

Hamish remembered this was code for Known Whereabouts.

One of the suspects, Bruno Concha Mendoza, nicknamed in the gang as "Bruiser," was identified as living at a residence south of San Diego, in Imperial Beach, very close to the San Ysidro border crossing.

Rodney dispatched a team of four to conduct a raid. He made his call first and got permission from the president.

Joachim Alvarez was the younger brother of another known gang member, and they had locations for the older brother. Rodney's team was researching others.

The vehicle they used was found abandoned in a commercial warehouse district—a maze of semis and shipping containers, and had been stolen from a car dealership lot. He had SDPD seize it and tow it to their FBI task force facility, searching for prints or other evidence. Rodney said they'd get results in less than an hour.

"I'd like to go on those raids. Is it too late to attach to the one for Bruno?" Hamish asked. "I can bring along a couple of guys."

Rodney Carson peered over at him. Hamish could tell he was about to tell him no.

"I got to do something, man. I can't just sit here

and wait. I don't do wait very well."

The agent nodded, walked over to a woman manning a coms desk. "Can you patch me through?"

"Sure, sir." She handed him the speaker.

"Hey, Bryce? I got a couple ride-alongs."

The radio was full of static, but in-between, Hamish could hear swearing.

"He's the father of the little girl, man. Former Navy SEAL, and he's fully vetted by the White House. Where are you?"

Reluctantly, the raid captain agreed to allow just one, and Hamish was given coordinates to meet the task force.

Harper pulled him aside just before he left. "Keep it holstered. We don't need you bounced."

Hamish was going to argue but stopped himself. "Roger that."

He ran down the stairs and out to his truck, plugged in the address to his GPS and headed straight for the highway. He had a twenty-minute drive, if there wasn't traffic.

There were four of them, dressed in unmarked tactical gear. Introductions were very brief. They tossed him a vest.

"You got a hat?" Pat Krebs asked.

Hamish retrieved his Punisher hat from the truck, locked it, and jumped into the second seat of the second vehicle, a black Hummer, again, with no markings.

There was no chitchat along the way. No jokes. He knew that was normal. They didn't know him. He was clearly an outsider, and he hadn't proven himself, no matter how vetted he was. They wanted him to know they were taking on danger by having him come along. They wanted him to know they only did it because they were told to by their superior.

Arriving at the address, they surveilled the area then put up a tiny Deca-Drone. Circling the property, it gave them a bird's eye view of the surrounding properties. It appeared there was a large dog who occupied the rear of the property, based on a worn path and presence of a large dog house and chain leading into it.

"These fuckin' guys always have dogs. I hate to kill a dog," one of the team said.

"Let me take the dog," said Hamish.

They chuckled at that. "We owe that to you. So go ahead, if you have to."

Vehicles outside and in the carport were registered to family members, but not to Bruno himself. Hamish hopped the fence with two other members, as two pounded on the front door and requested entry.

With no answer, they broke the door down. The two in the rear were able to walk right in. It was unlocked.

A large growling white-and-grey spotted pit bull stood in the doorway of his dog house, looking very territorial. Hamish took aim but landed his shot on the ground in front of the dog, kicking up dirt. The huge pup sat, which surprised him.

"You're a very smart dog," he whispered back to the canine.

They brought out the three occupants, two men and a woman. The woman appeared underage and did not speak English. The other two claimed to be just roommates, not related to Bruno, said they rented the house from the family.

Their English was good enough to ask questions about Sasha. Pat showed her photo, and both men shook their heads.

But they were all tied and hauled back to the task force building, including the young girl. Hamish guessed she had been trafficked from Mexico or Central America.

"Okay, gents," Pat said. "One down, a hundred more to go."

That was a chilling thought. What if they didn't get the right location in time? But although it was a dried-up lead, at least it was a lead.

And the dog lived.

CHAPTER 12

ANGIE WOKE UP from a sound sleep to a noise coming from downstairs. She reached for her Sig, checked to make sure it was fully loaded, tucked it in the pocket of her robe, and tiptoed down the hall to Cora's room. She was fast asleep, even snoring. She had stripped off her uniform, left her clothes in a pile at the foot of the bed, and apparently never showered. Angie picked them up, finding her smelly socks too, and was going to take them to the wash.

She passed by Sasha's room, with her gym bag sitting idly on her bed. Her heart felt like it had a fishhook in it. She tore her eyes away and continued to the top of the stairs, peering down to see if one of the men was on the couch.

It was Luke. He'd fallen off the couch, but to be sure, she quietly stepped down barefoot until she could see he was still breathing and apparently not injured.

As she turned on her heel to make it to the washer

in the garage, a hand reached out from under the covers and grabbed her ankle.

She dropped the clothes and fell to the floor sideways, skinning one knee. She kicked and screamed. The hand would not let go.

Suddenly, Brian barged into the room with his weapon drawn, pointed right at her. After a split second focused on the lump on the floor, he stood down.

"Chrissakes, Luke. Let go of Mrs. McDougall's leg, you dumb ass."

The other team member pushed the covers from his head, raised up, saw his hand clutched around Angie's ankle, and quickly withdrew as if her flesh were made of molten lead.

"Oh God. Not again. So sorry, ma'am."

Angie righted herself, brushing her robe down, checking to make sure her gun hadn't left her pocket, and got herself composed. She heard Cora at the top of the stairs.

"Mom! Are you all right?"

"I'm fine!"

"Not your mom's fault. My bad," said Luke.

"Go back to bed, Cora. I'm going to put your uniform in the wash. I'll be up in a bit."

Without looking at the two deflated and no doubt embarrassed warriors, she stepped into the garage and turned on the wash. She added lavender scent.

"Ma'am, we'd appreciate it if you didn't tell your husband. We're trying to get on the team, and we don't need this."

"I don't need it either. My daughter is missing, but you're glad I didn't pull this out." She showed them her Sig.

They both whistled.

"Kind of dangerous for you. Luke, if you can't control your nightmares or whatever it was, you'll have to sleep outside, I'm afraid."

"Yes, ma'am. No problem."

"Stay there for now. Brian, you'd better get outside and see if anyone was bothered by my scream. That'll be the next thing."

"Yes, ma'am."

Angie climbed the stairs, even more tired than she was before. She hadn't heard from Hamish, and that concerned her. She had wanted Sasha not to have to spend a night with her captors. She wanted her home, safe. She wanted her complete family around her.

It was barely ten. After she tucked Cora back in her bed, she returned to the master and picked up her phone again. She decided to see if Lydia was still up and texted her.

The answer came back right away. She was nursing, but she'd call when the baby went back to sleep.

About a half hour later, her phone rang.

"I didn't mean to interrupt you, Lydia."

"Not to worry, sweetie. How are you feeling? I would never turn down a call from you, especially with what's gone on. I haven't heard from Harper since this afternoon when he left."

"I saw the tape, Lydia. I saw her being dragged away. We think they drugged her. She could barely walk." The tears coming hurt her eyes, they were so sore from crying. "This waiting is hell on me. I feel so helpless. I know they're good at what they do, but there are so many mistakes that could be made, so many little details they have to look over. The mother in me makes me want to stay down there and make a complete pest of myself. But they're right to send me home. Wish I could take advantage of it."

"I understand completely. I wouldn't be able to settle down, either. Just talk to me. Tell me the whole story. Maybe that will make you feel better."

She left off the part about Luke grabbing her leg in his sleep but went through her whole day, the arrival at the complex, all the noise, the people, the confusion. She even went into her discussions with Marie. Lydia took exception to those.

"Has he been checked out, her husband?"

"Well, they know about him. And Hamish was going to have a check ran, but that was before Sasha wound up missing. It's probably all my imagination, Lydia."

"Of all the people I know, I wouldn't suspect you of fighting windmills. You've got a good head on your shoulders. I'd insist. Don't give up. Play your hunches. You want me to mention something to Harper?"

"He's already got a lot on his plate. Hamish, I know, is distracted, probably wondering which way to go. This whole thing blew up their op, totally."

"And now they're adjusting. That's what they do. The enemy gets a vote. They plan, and then when it goes to hell, they use the backup plan."

"Yeah, but in this case, I don't think there was one. Who knew they would do this?"

"Which is all the reason you need to get them focused on Marie's husband. Someone has a connection to your family, Angie. I don't think even the bad guys are that lucky."

She was right, of course.

They talked further and then signed off. She promised to update Lydia in the morning. Now at least, she could face the night.

"Sweetheart, my dear sweet girl, be brave. Keep thinking. Keep looking for ways you can escape. Know that we are doing everything we can to get you home safe. Hope you can feel my love and know your mama would do anything to trade places with you. Can't wait to see you again, in happier times."

She couldn't help the tears, but she let them rest on her cheeks as she buried her head and dreamt of their homecoming, every single detail of it. It was sure to happen!

CHAPTER 13

HAMISH WAS MORE than glum when the team dropped him back at his truck. He checked in with Harper.

"Yeah, I heard all about it. Tough one. But you would have been a wreck if you didn't go. I know you, you big giant-slayer, you guy-who-tosses-trees. That would be your Dine name."

"Shut the fuck up, Harper. Give me a break. I'm exhausted."

"You know what it is, Hamish. You had too many pancakes this morning, and now you're fading. Go home. Go be with your wife."

"But what about the task force?"

"We're going to stay here through tomorrow, and then everything goes back to the Team building on base. We're still waiting for info on a possible data breach here."

"There's a leak?"

"No, the festival archives have been hacked. As in two thousand girls' names, addresses, and even phone numbers were on a database that went out there somewhere."

"How did that happen?"

"That's why we're here. The agents are rather keen on getting that information. Two of Rodney's guys are working with their data people, who came down from LA to help them out. It's not hard to hack these. Just need to know what you're looking for. Probably, they had weak passcodes or shared them somewhere, and it got sent to the dark web. These guys knew what they were looking for."

"So that means they have Cora's information, too, and Sasha's."

"More than likely."

"Well, home sounds good, but if you don't update me, every detail, Harper, I'll wring your neck. I'll weed whack your garden shorter than a Marine's haircut."

"Just try it. Venom will have something to say about that."

"Oh, did the guys show up?"

"They did. Danny, Armando, and Fredo. They said they might head off your way after I gave them the update. You mind the interference?"

"You mean, did I have any plans with my wife?"

"That, and I thought you might need the rest, sleep

off those carbs. Did you eat anything else but breakfast at the camp site today?"

"Some nuts. An energy bar."

"You know what? You head over to the house. I'll have them stop by with some grub. I'll pay for it, or it will come from our expense account. You wait up for them, you hear?"

"Yes, boss."

He texted Angie but got no response. He let her know he'd be coming home for the night.

She met him at the front door with her arms outstretched. He expected she'd be exhausted, as he felt. Her fresh face and warm smile sizzled all the way to his toes. God, how he loved her.

Before their embrace, he poured out his heart. "I look at you, and honest to God, I think you're more beautiful than the day we got married, and I was pretty tongue-tied that day, if you'll remember."

Her eyes sparkled. She lowered her arms and played along with his little pre-hug speech.

"I remember every second of that day, Hamish. One of the best of my life. You swept me off my feet, and look at you, you're still carrying me all these years later."

"For better or for worse," he said.

"In sickness and in health," she answered.

"Till—"

She covered his mouth with her hand and slammed her body against him, taking his head in her hands and kissing him hard while he pulled her into him and hung on as tight as he could. He wasn't able to get enough of her. He had planned to be a forever bachelor, even before joining the Teams, and with that one look that first day they were introduced at the beach in San Diego, she blew all that up. He had never been the same again. Nor did he want to be anything other than the man she loved. If he could earn that, his life was perfect.

They both had tears in their eyes when they parted, the emotions and the connection between jointly shared and sweetly showered upon them both. Yes, it was sad what they were going through. But they had *this*. And with *this*, all things were possible.

"The team is right behind me, sweetheart. I'd love to really more properly show you how much I love you, but there isn't time."

"I've got the rest of my life, Hamish. And what they're helping us do is important. Right now, it's important. When we find her, we'll have room for other things. I know we will."

"Ever faithful, aren't you, my love?"

"What else could I be? It's who we are. Ordinary people doing extraordinary things."

"The odds are with us, Angie."

"We make the odds. We destroy obstacles."

A brand new red four-door Hummer parked right in front of their house. Out popped Fredo behind the wheel, waving to Luke and Brian as he ran up the meandering path to the porch, with Danny and Armando behind him, each carrying bags of hot food.

"I hope you had sex before," said Fredo. "Because after this shit, you're going to feel too fat, my man!"

Hamish exchanged a glance at his wife.

"He's wrong," she whispered and then giggled.

"You guys want to come in and join us?" Hamish extended to Luke and Brian, who agreed.

Angie set out plates and silverware, brought out her red, white, and blue cloth napkins, and filled the table with sodas, waters, and beer. Everyone found a seat at once, passing things around, and scooping up the chile rellenos, the lobster mac and cheese, and pizza with every kind of meat possible on it.

"How many places did you stop at?"

"Two. Only two," said Danny, filling his face with pizza.

"Next time, I'll bring some of Mia's tamales," said Fredo. "I'm a lucky man. I get tamales with my eggs, tamales with my steak, and tamales for snack. Every day is the same."

"And when he goes over to Felicia's house, he eats tamales," said Armando.

Everyone laughed.

"My sister never cooked like this when she lived at home. She was too busy partying," Armando continued. "Fredo, you've always been the best influence on her."

"Smitten at first sight. Hopelessly devoted," said Danny. "Lovestruck."

"Hey, bear cub, you weren't on the Team yet," objected Fredo.

"Oh, but I heard plenty, trust me," Danny responded.

Hamish studied the guys from Team 3. "Times like these, I wish I'd picked Kyle's team. Feels like I missed so much."

"Every team is different," said Armando. "And they change. Kyle's over twenty years now. That's almost a record."

"We've gotten him in trouble more than he planned," said Fredo. "But thank God he's still here!"

"It's true," said Armando. "He's had some close calls with the Headshed. He was certain they were going to toss him several times."

Hamish had wanted to talk to Danny ever since their visit to the Navajo Nation. He decided this was his opportunity.

"Harper and I really appreciated the guided tour of the Navajo lands, Danny, and just a tiny glimpse of your culture."

"Always happy to do it when someone is genuinely interested."

"You guys probably know, they've lost a lot of their children over the years, victimized by con artists who promise them fame and fortune and then turn them into God knows what. I'm praying we get Sasha back. I just can't imagine that happening to her."

He was having a bit of trouble getting it out.

Angie put her hand on his folded on the table.

"When these children go missing, what's the first thing your people would do? Where would they look first?"

"Often, they have a friend or relative somewhere close to where they are going. Someone knows where they are going. We do the rounds of the hospitals, police stations. We drive the backroads and check abandoned buildings. But usually someone knows they have been planning something. This thing with Sasha is different. She may have been targeted, but, Hamish, I don't get that she'll be trafficked. I think it's something else. This is too high profile for them. There is a reason they chose her."

Armando agreed. "And for an abduction, coming to the Convention Center with all the people and cameras—there are lots easier ways to take a girl than do it there. This seems intentional, well planned, and like Danny said, more high profile. I don't think they will harm her. They want her for some reason."

"So you think ransom? We're not rich, Armando," said Hamish.

"Not ransom, but something else."

"You think the task force? The Silver Team working on this project?"

Danny nodded. "That's my hunch. There's a leak somewhere."

Hamish searched his brain. Then he remembered something.

"What do you remember about Connor Brown? He was on SEAL Team 3 with you guys, right?"

"He was. He was an okay guy. Kept to himself, but he did his job," said Danny.

"One of those guys who didn't have a family, so he didn't come to the parties, even the all-adult parties. Kind of a loner," said Fredo.

"I know he liked to gamble," said Armando. "He used to gamble at the Indian casinos in the valley."

"Hmm. That surprises me. I've met him a few times, but Marie, his wife, is Angie's best friend."

Angie spoke up. "She's been a great friend. She stuck by me all day today."

"Wait. She was there today? At the Convention Center?" asked Danny.

"Yes, I invited her. Why?"

"Maybe she told someone she shouldn't have?" Hamish asked. "They don't seem like the kind of people who would be involved with something like this. He's hard to get close to, but Marie isn't that way at all."

"No, not at all. She didn't like the interview with the FBI today. They asked her about her husband's job. Got that idea from Hamish," said Angie.

"Why did you have them ask about that?" Danny wanted to know.

"Marie told Angie he worked as a consultant for some NGO's, and it has something to do with immigration, too. You didn't tell her anything about my job, did you, honey?" Hamish asked.

"Generalities. She asked me, and I was vague."

"I asked Rodney, he runs the special agent pool, to check him out. He should have that by now."

"Well, it's something to just watch for now," said Armando.

"We know the guys who took her, and they are criminals, and they deal with the kidnappings and trafficking, according to the Feds. They are worker bees. They work for the big bosses," said Hamish. "We find them, we get their bosses."

Angie's phone rang. It was an unknown number, like one of those that showed up when Hamish was overseas and needed to call home. Encrypted.

"Hello?" She stood and started to walk into the kitchen. Then she stopped.

"It's Sasha!" she whispered. "Just a minute, honey. Your Dad's here. Let me put it on speaker."

They all heard her small voice.

"Mama, come get me. I'm scared."

"Where are you?" asked Hamish, suddenly sitting up, grabbing his cell, and recording her voice.

"I snuck out when one of the guards left my cell open. They have us in shipping containers. There are lots of us. But they put me by myself."

"Are you inside a container now?"

"No, I escaped. I climbed over the fence before the dogs came out. They send dogs after kids who try to run away. Daddy, come get me please."

"Sweetheart, give me a little help. What does it look like there?"

"It's dark. I can't see."

"Any signs, any sounds you recognize?"

They heard a whistle blow in the distance.

"Is there a train? Near train tracks?"

"Yes, I think so. Lots of fencing. Warehouses and stacks of shipping containers. I'm at a road, a dirt road. There are four cars here and a big semi parked next to them."

"Can you hear the ocean?"

"No."

"Hear any airplanes?"

"Maybe one. A small one?"

"Is it close by?"

"I don't think so. Oh, wait. I see a sign. The building next to the containers has a sign in blue. It says Nevada Home. Underneath it, there's a number all lit up. Number nine-two-five."

Hamish started searching the internet and Google maps, calling up the name, and found a warehouse listed as Nevada Home.

"Got it. Jesus, it's not more than a mile from the home we raided."

"Someone's coming," Sasha's voice whispered.

"See if you can hide near the tires of the big rig, honey. Are they driving or walking?"

"Walking. Two men."

They listened as they heard footsteps on gravel. The men were speaking Spanish. Fredo translated.

"He's saying that after this run he's going to go looking for a little place by the beach down near San Felipe. He was going to call for his wife to come up to meet him there at Christmastime."

"There's a bigger group next week."

"So they will wait to send these off?"

"No, the boat arrives tomorrow. They don't hang around very long. Not that long."

At last, the footsteps faded.

"Sasha, are you there?" Hamish whispered.

"Yes," she whispered back. "Daddy, I'm real scared."

"Honey, we know right where you are. Hide around the tires. Don't let anyone see you. Maybe lean up against and try to stay warm. I know right where you are. I'll be there in less than a half hour. Hang on. Be brave, Sasha. We love you so much."

"I love you too, Daddy."

When Hamish stood up, Danny, Fredo, and Armando did as well. "Well, I guess we're all going."

They dashed out of the house, taking Fredo's new red Hummer, which didn't look quite so bright in the night air. Hamish's phone rang. It was Harper.

"Going to need you boys back here."

"Harper, Sasha called us. I think I know where she is. We're going to go get her."

"We?"

"I have Danny, Armando, and Fredo."

"No firefight. I'll get a small team to meet you over there. Text the info to me."

"We're not waiting, Harper. They can come, but we're engaging. We'll try to keep it legal." He texted Harper the address number and general coordinates. He also sent the electronic footprint of the phone she was calling from. "Haven't found a street name yet, but we searched the name Nevada Home."

"Wait, she's outside the perimeter?"

"Yes, she managed to escape. I don't think they know she's missing."

"Roger that. But there's one other thing, the reason I called. We found the priest about an hour ago. Cut his throat from ear to ear, poor man. No laptop found anywhere."

"Where did this happen?"

"He was working at his charity office."

"Where was his detail?"

"That's the thing. There were no signs anyone entered or left the building. He was working alone. It's like they just came in and out without a trace. Rodney has a team over there, assisting the police. We're ready to raid some other houses, but you go get Sasha first. Sounds like the warehouse district from your description."

He updated the others on the conversation.

"They're plugging leaks. Cleanup has started." Armando whistled.

Which made Hamish consider Sasha would be their next focus of attention, and that thought petrified him.

"You need me in position?" Danny asked him, wondering if he should set up his sniper cage.

"I'd rather have you man-to-man. I say we grab her and worry about picking up the pieces later. That okay with you fellas? Harper said no firefight. We pick them off, someone's gonna pay for that. Got to keep the collateral down."

"Sounds good to me," said Fredo. Others agreed.

They drove slowly down one side street, after turning of the expressway, onto partially paved but heavily potholed roads covered in gravel, extinguishing their lights. Most of the warehouses were fenced with chainlink and razor wire, with multiple bright lights mounted, probably with sensors and cameras. Only a few had security guard stations, but they didn't see any that were manned since most businesses were shut down and used for loading and unloading cargo vans and boxcars. With Fredo's blackout windows, they might catch a break and not get discovered until they were on their way out.

Looking down each street as they passed, Hamish was searching for the semi and several cars nearby, something Sasha had mentioned. Their first pass through yielded nothing.

"Dammit. Should have brought Angie's phone."

"You want me to synch them?" asked Armando.

"No, Angie will call me if she tries to contact again. I wouldn't risk a ringtone anyway."

"Listen, Hamish. It just so happens Danny and I brought some firecrackers, some little flash bombs that make a lot of noise. I got heavier stuff if you want to blow shit up. My bag's behind you. I should bring it, yes?"

"Hell, let's make a party out of it, once we locate her."

"Wish I had one of Coop's little cute drones. They could drop a little surprise on them."

"Can you place and time them?"

"I got a couple. But they're destructive. You'll wake up half of Imperial Beach."

"Noted. Let's find that semi first, but yeah, you get them ready when we park."

Danny held up his slingshot and smiled.

"God, hope we don't have to get that close, but good on you, Danny," said Harper.

"Nice if we had something other than ammo vests. Didn't think we'd need those," said Armando.

"But I'm assuming everyone's got their sidearm?" asked Hamish.

Several in the group had two. Danny had brought his M3, which was already strapped to his body.

As they crossed in the other direction, scanning down streets that went east to west, Hamish spotted a semi parked outside a fenced enclosure with several cars parked nearby, all appearing unoccupied. Fredo pulled over and shut the engine.

Hamish didn't have to give any instructions. In pairs, they took both sides of the street, searching all directions, as they passed the parked cars until they approached the semi.

"Sasha?" Hamish whispered.

"I'm here, Dad," came the weak little voice.

"Can you slide out and follow my voice. I'm on the streetside, not near the fence."

Several seconds later, her face appeared and then one of her long arms, as he and Danny pulled her from under the trailer. Her face was smeared with grime. She'd been smart and used her knee pads to protect herself while crawling. She had small cuts on her forehead, a bruised cheekbone, and a welt and serious gash on her forearm with dried blood. Her jersey, still with her number eight attached, was ripped in places and part of the team logo was detaching from one of those. And of course she was still wearing her spandex, so her thighs were scratched with tiny cuts. Her pony tail was askew, her ribbons long gone. Hamish picked up the distinct odor of urine.

She dove into his arms. It felt so good to hold her tall, skinny, shivering frame.

"You okay? Anything broken? Did they hurt you in any way?"

"No, Daddy. I got bruises on my arms where they yanked me around. Everything will heal. Take me home. Get me out of here."

"We got you, sweetheart."

Danny spoke. "We got incoming. Two men walking along the perimeter headed toward Fredo's truck." He slipped into the darkness, Armando behind him, covering him with his sidearm.

Hamish and Fredo pulled Sasha away from the light into a dark pocket in front by the cab. One car was parked facing the wrong direction on the street but also gave them a dark patch if they needed it.

They heard sounds of a scuffle but only a whispered "sonofabitch" as one of Danny's rocks apparently landed on someone's forehead and sounded like it could have cracked his skull.

Armando whistled the all-clear, and the three ran toward the red vehicle. Fredo swore as he accidentally hit the lock button on his key fob. His headlights flashed, and the alarm made a little "whoop" sound.

Lights came on behind one of the fences, and they could see three men running toward them.

"We got company, gents. Get us out of here, Fredo."

Everyone loaded, Fredo tore off down the street so fast he began to fishtail back and forth, just narrowly missing sideswiping another gate. He turned the corner too quickly and did sideswipe part of the fence.

"Fuckin' Hell. My brand-new truck, God dammit!"

Suddenly, the road ended. It did not go through. They had to double back or snake their way out on another street. The GPS on the dash was too bright, and he'd turned it off.

"Turn right at the corner. I think that goes through," said Armando from the passenger seat.

Sasha clung to Hamish, shivering while he stroked her hair, placed his jacket over her shoulders, and held her hands between his to warm them. "You're going to be okay, Sasha. We're going home now."

She didn't answer but squeezed him harder.

They could see the busy expressway beyond, so Fredo sped up just as two gunmen appeared in the middle of the street, aiming right at them.

"Fuck this. Get one of those things," he said to Armando, who dug for one of the flashes. He rolled down the window, pulled the pin, and lobbed it forward, landing between the two, and then Fredo gunned it again.

The flash stunned them, but not until one of them hit the truck with a spray of shot which arched over his hood but missed everyone in the front seat. If his aim had been any better, he could have wiped out everyone in the back seat.

Fredo hit the shooter head-on, and the man went flying. The other lay wounded on the ground.

They hit the expressway and barreled north.

Hamish wasn't paying much attention to the jabbering Fredo was having in Spanish with Armando, who obviously was trying to calm him down. Of course, he knew the truck would be fully repaired.

Then he remembered the team headed over to the warehouse. He quickly called Harper and told him they had Sasha. The team could stand down.

"You did great, kid," said Danny. "You kept your cool. I'm impressed. You got street smarts. How did you ever get away?"

"I picked the lock on the cage."

"You what?" asked Hamish.

"I picked the lock. We learned it at church camp."

Hamish sighed, struggling with this new factoid he should forget about, but he just couldn't let it go.

"You know how to pick locks? And why did they teach that to you at camp. A church camp?"

"I dunno. One of the kids taught us. It was cool. Very easy."

"What did you use?"

"One of my hair clips. I have pink sparkly ones. They stayed in really well."

That got Fredo's attention off the condition of his brand-new truck.

"Oh, I can see that family conversation now. Oh yes, I'd give anything to listen to that one. Hamish, your kids are just like you. Even better!"

He laughed as he drove like a bat out of Hell.

Armando blurted a reprimand. "Fredo, would you

watch your driving? You are cop bait right now. Driving a brand-new red Humvee with bullet holes all over the hood and a scraped rear side panel doing, what, twenty over the speed limit at midnight? With tinted windows. Think, man, how that looks!"

Hamish didn't care. As long as they were on their way home, nothing was going to upset him.

CHAPTER 14

D ANNY AND HAMISH helped Sasha up the steps to the front porch of her home then helped her through the doorway and into the arms of her mother, where she burst into tears, sobbing.

Angie's back stood firm as the lanky teen leaned all her weight against her.

"Sweetheart, we're so happy you're home. Welcome home, honey. You were brave. You were so brave, Sasha. You hear me? Really good thinking on your part."

"Mom, I was so scared. And I think about the other girls. There are children all over that warehouse, stored in cages, tied up. It was awful. They were taking naked pictures. Everyone was crying. Nobody cared for these kids, Mom."

Angie stared at Hamish, that unspoken command to make sure someone knew about this and was going to do something about it. He nodded his response, and picked up the phone, walking outside to the porch. The door was ajar, and she could hear him talking.

Luke and Brian congratulated him.

"Don't let your guard down. They might send a whole army over here next. We're not out of the woods yet. In fact, I'm going to call for more backup."

"Roger that," said Luke.

Sasha must have heard it as well. She jerked free of her mother and stared at the front door. "Are they coming? Are they really coming?" she said, horrified.

"Sweetheart, he was just telling Luke and Brian— they're dad's guys—telling them to be careful. Just because you're home, which is the hard part, we still need to protect ourselves. But look who we have here? These men, along with your dad, saved your life tonight, sweetheart. But the work isn't done. Your father is going to get those assholes." She bowed her head. "Sorry."

"Mom. You don't have to apologize to me. I was being stupid."

Armando put his hand on her shoulder carefully. "May I?" he asked permission to speak to her. Angie nodded, and holding Sasha, turned in Armando's direction.

"Look, you did so well, Sasha. But think about it. You witnessed something, and now all that information is going to be given to the task force to deal with it. You have all that valuable information. We aren't going anywhere until this process is complete. Until then, you're still under our protection. The job's not done. He was reminding them of that."

She nodded. "Thank you. You're right. You're Armando, right?" she asked.

"Yes."

"I used to babysit for you and Gina when Artemis was—" She stopped, her eyes filling up with tears.

"It's okay. I'm remarried now. Artemis has a new mom and a new brother. I'll have to introduce you sometime."

"I was so sorry—"

"It's okay, Sasha. Life goes on, doesn't it? Your dad, his whole life is wrapped up in you guys, you four and Angie here. He'd do anything to protect you, wouldn't he? He'd never stop. I'm the same way. Artemis helped me with that after Gina was gone. Our kids are everything, and always will be."

Angie had admired Armando for years, watching all the changes in his life. He was a legend on Team 3, as Hamish was to Team 5.

But as she watched Fredo begin to mumble about his truck, Danny patiently listening, she realized they all were legends. They all were capable of extraordinary things. They all were the best of the best.

"Can I get cleaned up?"

"I want to wait on that. Not sure if we should do that. Part of this, when you've become a victim, is that everything has to be documented. I think we should wait until the investigators let us know. Let me get you a blanket. If I wash that uniform and you shower, all the evidence will be washed away."

"But, Mom, I wasn't raped."

"Sasha, it's a hard no. I don't want to do anything that will interfere with what has to be done to get these guys behind bars. That's the goal."

She knew by Sasha's body language she hadn't been sexually assaulted. But she was more than happy to hear it coming from Sasha's own voice.

Armando smiled. "You mom's right. Smart lady, like you, Sasha." He patted her on the back.

Angie brought in a fuzzy blanket, one of her favorites, and wrapped her in it. "Have you eaten anything since this morning?"

She shook her head and sat down on the couch.

"What do you want?"

"Corn flakes?"

"Corn flakes. What about a meal, like a mac and cheese or grilled cheese sandwich?"

"Cornflakes and milk."

"Okay." She ran to the kitchen and brought back the bowl. Sasha dove into it, famished.

"Sasha!" came Cora's voice at the top of the stairs.

She ran down toward her sister, and the two embraced, both crying. Angie started to cry again as well.

"Are you okay? Did they…?"

"No, I'm fine. But it was horrible. They have other children there, mostly younger than I am. In cages, Cora. Kept them in cages like animals."

"Who were these men?" she asked.

"Some bad guys. I didn't understand most of what they said because very few spoke English. Look at me, Cora. I'm a mess."

That made her sister giggle. "New costume for Halloween. Zombie volleyball player!"

"Stop that. Not funny," Sasha frowned.

"Cora, you know better than that," Angie added.

"Okay, I'm sorry. I truly am. Just trying to cheer you up a bit. Thank goodness for Dad and his big hunky guys, huh?"

"Cora, you shouldn't talk about them like that," said Sasha.

"You should talk. That big old crush on Harper and all," she said, lowering her voice. Armando had walked over to Fredo and Danny.

"Girls. Time for that is later."

"You want some?" Sasha asked Cora, holding up a spoonful of flakes and milk.

"No. I just wanted to say hi. I'm going to play tomorrow—well, it's Sunday now, so today. I need to get back to bed."

"You sleep in, Cora. We'll talk about this in the morning," Angie inserted. "Nothing is for sure."

They hugged, and Cora left the room.

"Want another?"

"Could I have water? And I need to pee. I'm stinky, I know. They wouldn't let us go to the bathroom, so…"

"Of course. I know it sounds odd, but don't wash your hands. You're wearing evidence all over you, sweetheart. But absolutely, go use the restroom."

She held Sasha's half-finished cereal, waiting for the next shoe to drop. Now that this was resolved, she was beginning to feel really tired and in need of some restorative rest.

Later, after the forensics unit left, she sent Sasha upstairs to finally shower. Her clothes were bagged and taken. It would be a while before she'd get her uniform back, but they'd put a rush on it, they said.

Angie checked her watch. It was nearly one o'clock.

CHAPTER 15

H AMISH TRIED TO be quiet. He'd finished a long conversation with Harper then sent Danny, Armando, and Fredo to their own homes.

"I owe you guys a solid. Thanks. If you hadn't been here, I'd be still waiting on that team to let us know."

"Are they going to raid tonight?" asked Armando.

"I don't know. Harper says they might, but they got a lot going on."

"Well, you tell him, if they need more bodies, I'm available. Kyle okayed anything we could do to help out, as long as we don't get injured, of course," said Armando.

Danny and Fredo agreed.

"Listen," said Danny. "You need to ask Harper about Connor. If he has anything to do with this organization, he could be sitting good for a murder investigation. Would be a good time for a change of heart."

"I thought of that as well. But what if he's not?"

"Don't take chances you don't have to take, Hamish," Fredo added. "Danny's right."

"Okay, I'll get on it in the morning. Fellas, thanks is never enough. You are truly my brothers."

"Likewise. Don't be a stranger. And no more ditching our bonfires. You're one of us now!"

He loved hearing that as he watched them dance their way down the steps and into Fredo's totally messed up truck.

He'd forgotten to mention that to Harper. They needed to add an expense report for that estimate.

He said good night to Luke and Brian and handed them his remote for the alarm.

"Anything at all happens, you hit this. We'll have lights, camera, action, and some screaming like you've never heard before. I'm not going to demonstrate or I'll have to move. Just push it once, and a notice gets sent straight to SDPD."

"Cool. Never seen one of these."

"Not commercially available. Coop rigged it for me. He's nuts for gadgets."

Leaving them both on the porch, he locked the front door and checked all the windows and the back door, plus the living room slider. He still had the feeling there were eyes on him. But he needed rest. And there were half a dozen men he could call who would be there in ten minutes. And God forbid he woke up hearing that alarm.

"But whatever it takes," he whispered to himself.

Removing his shoes, he tiptoed up the stairs and down the hall to the bedroom, passing Sasha and Cora's bedrooms. He left the doors open so he could hear anything stirring.

Angie was fast asleep, snoring like a sailor, as he'd told her so many times, and she denied it every time she heard it. Even took offense at it.

He slipped into the shower and quickly got all the dust and grime of the day washed away. He could finally breath, the warm mist so freeing.

Drying off, he bent over the countertop, his fingers bracing his upper torso. In the mirror, he didn't recognize the man he'd become. He'd aged ten years. His heart had been yanked back and forth, his guts jumbled so many times he had almost lost it several times during the day. This morning, he'd cooked pancakes for the boys at the beach, the gentle sounds of the waves and the birds drowning out all the sounds of the city, of his blood-spattered dreams, of his worries and his old age aches and pains. Just sitting on the sand in those bright chairs Angie bought, the three men of the family, eating pancakes, was about as right as it could be. He'd be a different man if he could have more days like that. Nothing planned and not expecting danger.

It was almost Heaven.

But Heaven was waiting for him with outstretched arms as he slipped into bed naked and held Angie. She was always the very best part of him, connected in every single way except one, and that was going to be remedied soon. Like they used to do when they were young and first married, maybe they'd sleep that way, sweaty and connected.

She needed his rough kisses, begged for him to go deep, couldn't get enough of all of it, which only spurred him on more. This hairless creature, so strong and yet so delicate, brought him to his knees as he worshiped her, kissed her everywhere he could find, and staked his claim to her soul. She was his. She was his lifeblood and his reason for living.

There was no such thing as loving someone too much.

MORNING CAME TOO quickly. He grabbed his pajama bottoms stuffed into his pillowcase and made his way downstairs, where he smelled coffee brewing. Luke was at the table having a couple of eggs with her.

"Mornin'," he said.

Her bright smile piqued his libido again as she kissed him. "Mornin'. Coffee?"

"Yes, ma'am."

He sat down hard. She presented a steaming mug of his favorite Bone Frog Coffee in front of him.

"Fresh ground," she winked.

"Of course it is. Thanks, sweetheart."

"Well," Luke said as he pushed away from the table. "I'll relieve Brian so he can catch some grub. Thanks a bunch, Mrs. McDougall."

"Why can't I stop you boys from calling me that? It's Angie. Please. I call you by your first names."

"Yes, ma'am. Thank you, Angie."

"Take your mug with you. Should I refill it?"

"No, it was hot. I was waiting for it to cool."

"Not if you put enough half and half in it," Hamish grumbled. "That's what it's for."

"Oh, I drink it black, sir."

He growled like a troll. "Mother, we have a non-believer in our midst," he said with his Scottish accent.

"Well," Angie added, "If you get tired of waiting, you can always come in for a shot. You really should try it. You'd love the taste."

"I just might do that, ma'am. Thanks again."

He was out the door with his mug. In the same breath, Brian arrived, his face full of joy. "First, I have to use the restroom, if that's all right with you two?"

"Be sure to use the spray, Brian. We have ladies who live here, in case your innards are halfway like mine," chuckled Hamish.

Angie frowned. "Eggs and bacon?"

"Absolutely. I'll be right back."

"And here's yours, King of Good Times."

"That was a rather special time, last night, wasn't it? I'm hoping for a repeat performance tonight, if you're free."

"Let me clear my calendar, then, big boy," she whispered and kissed him.

Brian was embarrassed he'd interrupted the kiss. He sat down to his plate. It took a minute or two, but the smell of the lavender spray eventually wafted over to the table.

HARPER HAD SPENT the night down at the complex with Rodney and a couple others who were still going over street and building videos. He told Hamish they'd raided two of the designated houses, but the big score, of course, was the raid on the warehouse where they rescued forty-four girls and five young boys. The whole place had been in the process of packing up and moving out rapidly when the team arrived.

Harper told him that many of the children had been assaulted already, and none of them were coming to family members in the States. They were all going to sponsors, and they were able to retrieve the computers and some hard drives containing lists of names. Since they were unaccompanied minors, they got quick and fast processing. All of them had documents created by the Nevada House. There was even a certificate for Sasha, although they'd called her Sylvia with no last name, but it contained her stressed and frightened picture attached.

Eleven men were arrested under child trafficking charges, which required they be held shackled and confined in I.C.E. detention facility built just for this purpose. Lawyers were on their way, Harper told him.

Rodney's team was trying to make sure the children were kept together, clothed, and examined for abuse and illnesses, while relatives back home were being contacted or a suitable charity they trusted could be found.

"Problem is, most places are full up. And we want to make sure and vet the group that gets them," Harper continued.

"I'm glad. Sasha will be pleased to hear they've been picked up and are being looked after. She was worried about them."

"Rodney says they'll be working on the case from Washington, going to leapfrog over some jurisdictions here that might be compromised."

"That's a shame."

"Not all of them, probably not most of them. But we don't want to lose these kids in the system, and it's been happening all too frequently. The president himself says he might fly out here and meet with them. How about that?"

"I liked him before. I'm liking him even better now. Using his power for good. Amen to that," said Hamish. "So is the festival still on?"

"It is. But we're packing up here and going to move to the Team building. It's more secure, and we aren't in the way."

"What about the data breach?"

"They're checking with their lawyers. From a PR standpoint, you might begin to see that as a nightmare in the making. I have a strong opinion on the matter, as I'm sure you do, Hamish, but we can't make them do what they won't do."

"Until the parents sue. Someone's got an attorney in the family. It won't end that way."

"Let's just say I'm glad I'm not on their board."

"Cora wants to play today. If I bring a couple guys as lookouts, because Angie's going to stay here with Sasha and the boys are coming home, would you advise against it? She's dead set on playing. I tried to talk her out of it, so did Angie."

"I think that will work out. But your whole family is going to need to stay under protection. You bring her over, and I've got two guys, they're recruits, not yet graduated, who can do that detail. Then they'll bring her home, if that's okay."

"Perfect. Angie will like that. Cora won't mind a bit, being escorted home by two Special Forces recruits. That will make her day."

"As I thought it would."

"You need me right away? She's got the afternoon pool."

"I was going to say. The teams are already here, practicing. She'd be late. But come in an hour or two before. That would be—"

"Noon?"

"That's fine. Be with your girls and your best girl, Hamish. We're going to have to set up interviews so we can tape her testimony and get the warrants we're going to need. The president wants to go after the senator posthaste."

"As I said, my kind of guy."

Neil brought the boys home about an hour later. The kids were chattering, jumping up and down, hugging each other. They avidly listened to Sasha tell the tale of the events. Hamish was so grateful her trauma was mostly psychological and she hadn't been molested. Still the trauma would sneak up on her, and at times, she'd stop, coming to tears.

He also noticed how children who cared and were compassionate toward each other, had been taught to love, were so good for each other. They bantered lightly then quietly explored the darkness of the event, just talking, asking questions, and supporting Sasha. He was proud of how they'd raised them, and again, so grateful to Angie.

She caught him watching them out by the pool.

"You wouldn't know, would you?" she whispered.

"God, Angie. That was a close one. I wasn't sure there for a few. We'll need to all have some counseling to help process this. But look at them. Look at how good they are for her. You remember all the fights and arguments they sometimes have? Not today. Total love. I'm in awe."

His eyes had welled up.

He couldn't say it, but he felt he didn't deserve it.

"This is all you, Hamish. You've been teaching them since they were little to be resilient, be aware of their surroundings, treat others with respect. We've had some major lapses, and I'm going to remind Sasha that part about going to the restroom alone. The one thing she didn't tell us?"

"What's that?"

"She didn't tell us she gave up. You remember that? She told you the truth. She was afraid. She wanted to come home. She gave clear directions that helped get her home. She didn't panic. She did what she was taught. What you taught her, Hamish. It wasn't easy, but she held it together."

"No, Angie. That wasn't me. That was all her. She

has the heart of a lioness. They all are courageous, every one of them."

The two of them stood together watching their brood. Hamish knew it was going to be one of those days he'd remember for the rest of his life.

Luci called and asked if she could bring Ali over.

"He really wants to talk to Sasha. You know, he's been through a lot. He wants to talk to her. Would you mind?"

Hamish put his hand over the phone. "Ali wants to come over to talk to Sasha."

"I'm fine with that. As long as we all can hear it. All of us, Hamish."

He nodded and gave the okay.

When Ali arrived, he appeared nervous. Griffin and Chester were begging Luci to go into the pool, but she kept their hands and explained this wasn't a pool day, promising another to come.

"Wow," Ali said before he started, looking at the group. "I've never done public speaking before. So here goes."

The kids laughed.

"Sasha, I wanted to tell you that I'm so sorry for what happened yesterday. And you know it could have been worse." His face was serious as his eyes bored into her face.

Sasha nodded her head.

"Well, I've seen worse. I can't get those pictures out of my head. My doctor says I probably never will. I saw my father murdered. I wanted to run to him, to be with him, but they had him, and he wanted me to run away and get to safety."

Sasha began to cry. Ian tried to casually wipe a tear from his eye as well.

"I ran to my new father, Danny. He gave me the chance of a new life. It was what my father had always wanted, that we come here to the United States and live in freedom and peace."

Hamish held his breath. He wasn't certain where all this was going. He squeezed Angie's hand.

"But the truth is, Sasha. No place is completely safe. It never was. Children don't make it unsafe. Adults do. Adults do things, and we suffer. Children are suffering all over the world. Here too. That's not right, Sasha. I've been thinking a lot about this, even before yesterday, and I want, someday, to help the children not be unsafe. Will you help me because you understand now. Will you?"

Sasha smiled, still with tears in her eyes. She extended her hand and took his.

"I do understand, Ali. And I feel the same way. I don't know what I can do, but yes, I would like to help you."

Ian blurted out, "I want to help too."

"So do I," said Cora.

"Me too," said Andrew.

Angie said it best. "We all do. We'll be right there with you."

CHAPTER 16

A NGIE WAS MAKING preparations for dinner, watching the boys and Sasha play in the pool. Luci had brought over a huge pink dragon for Sasha and told her Ali wanted them to get it for her.

"For being a dragon-slayer."

They had set up a date to get Griffin and Chester their first pool party. Hamish and Cora were over at the Convention Center.

There was a knock at the door. She didn't get a text from Luke. Brian was out back, in his swim trunks, an old pair Hamish gave him, reading a book on the lounge chair.

She checked her phone again. A tall shadow stood in the doorway next to a shorter one.

She texted Luke. "Who's at the door?"

"Your friend, Marie, and her husband."

Angie felt her heartbeat begin to race. "Next time, tell me first."

She pushed her bangs off her face and opened the door with a smile.

Marie looked pained. Her eyes were red and puffy. Her fingers fidgeted with the loop on the side of her jeans.

"Angie, you remember Connor. Connor, this is Angie. Can we come in for a minute?"

Angie shook Connor's hand, sweaty and cold. He didn't look quite the picture of health he once had been. She'd seen pictures Marie had around the house, but he didn't resemble them at all.

"Have a seat. You want anything?"

"I'll take some water, please," Connor asked quickly.

"Marie?"

"Water's fine."

"Ice?"

"Yes, both of us a little ice please," Marie answered.

She handed them the two tumblers and sat in the rocking chair adjacent the couch where they sat side by side.

Marie examined her hands then looked sideways at Connor, expecting him to start. She took a big sip of water and set it beside her on the side table as she waited.

Finally, he spoke. "Angie, I've done some things I'm not very proud of recently. I wanted to come here to tell you what's been going on with us, and to, well, confess I've brought shame into our house."

Marie wouldn't make eye contact, and it was starting to concern Angie.

"Confess what?" She tried to act surprised, but inside, she really wasn't.

"Bottom line, the whole beginning of our problems started when I was on the Teams. We'd go out, the fellas and I, to have a few drinks. And some of us would go gambling. The Indian gambling places we liked the best. I told myself the odds were better, and all that. But the long and short of it is that I became a gambling addict."

"While you were a SEAL?"

"Yes, ma'am. I was warned a couple of times, but I told myself if I got out of the hole I'd dug, then I'd quit. I started borrowing money from some places I'm not proud of. I got hassled from time to time. But just about all my salary went into paying my debts. And I hid this from Marie."

Angie wondered where all this was leading.

"You're getting help for this?"

"I'm going to."

"How much are we talking about?" she asked.

"More than I had a chance to pay back, unless I won big. That's what I was going for. But I never did. No one ever does. It's rigged that way."

"But everyone knows this. Why did you do it?"

"It was just for fun at first, and then I had a rule that I would only lose so much. In the end, everything fell apart. I didn't voluntarily leave the Teams. I was asked to leave when it got reported. So I was offered a position when I detached, a position with one particular group out of Las Vegas, who agreed to wipe my debt clear if I promised not to gamble again, and that's what I did."

"Why would they make that kind of trade?" Angie asked.

"That's the point. What I should have figured out was they were investing in my future. I thought they were just being nice. I counseled their people on all things from firearm safety, shooting at the range, tactical procedures, how to set up a surveillance probe, and use of drones to how the different jurisdictions operate and to coordinate between police, fire, and the Sheriff's Department. All here in San Diego."

"Okay. So does this have anything to do with Sasha's ordeal? I just have to be blunt and ask you, Connor. Are we safe?"

She could see he didn't want to answer.

"Yes and no. They told me about Hamish working for this elite operation before you even told Marie about his new job. Might have even told me more things than you know. This surprised me, gave me a problem. You guys are my friends, a fellow brother. But even if that weren't the case, no one's family should be targeted like that."

"Why did they tell you this?"

"They told me there was a faction in their organization who were being hassled by ICE, State Department heads looking into the migrant charity we run. They sponsor summer kids' camps and baseball and basketball after school sports for minorities. But they also assist migrant unaccompanied minors to find good homes, sponsors, or family members in the U.S. who would take over responsibility for them, so they wouldn't be a burden on the taxpayers. I was training security personnel so the kids could be kept safe. It sounded okay, but I wondered, if it was legitimate. Why would they be bothered by the government, unless the government was dirty?"

"And you found out it wasn't legit."

"Exactly. And what's worse, they're making money, tons of money, from it. They even got a priest to help them. If you can't trust the clergy, who can you trust?"

"So why our family, Connor? I need to have the answer to that."

"Sasha was meant to be leverage, to get the team to back off and leave them alone. She was never going to be shipped off like the other kids they placed."

"Connor, they don't 'place' them. They basically

sell them to the highest bidder. They are trafficked, not given to better homes or any kind of home except brothels. And then they disappear. Just disappear. That's what they're in the business of." Angie couldn't hold it back any further. "How would they ever get away with this type of operation? This is the United States of America!"

"They have some kind of dirt on the president—I don't know what it is, but with these two things, they were trying to up their game, expand it. I was almost two years into this thing, and I found out all this. I'd been looking for a way out. I thought if maybe I came forward and told Hamish or Harper about what I knew that maybe Marie and I could get out from under their thumb. But then they murdered Father Flaherty. I knew that was going to happen to me. And then before I could find out how they were going to do it, they kidnapped Sasha."

Angie sat back in her chair. Her anger was getting the better of her. Marie had been her best friend.

"You knew!" she said to Marie.

"No, I never knew all this. I knew he had gambling debts. I knew he was working that debt off. I thought his training was all above-board. But, Angie, I swear to you, I never knew my husband worked for a human trafficking operation. He knows I would have told you. I knew he was working with migrant kids, helping them to find family and arrange travel to their destination."

"Haven't you been watching the news?"

"I never thought that was Connor's company. I never got that vibe," she said.

"But I did," said Connor. "I picked up on it right away when things started not adding up. I couldn't get an accounting of my gambling debts and how much had been worked off. I was working like a dog—six, sometimes seven days a week. They wanted me to move to Las Vegas, said they'd buy a car and a house for us, but none of those things started happening. I was duped. And then I was too afraid to quit. When they killed the priest, when they took Sasha, I decided I had to step forward to stop it."

"So what does all this mean?"

"I'm turning myself in. I want to help."

"Wait right there. I'm going to call Hamish."

Angie dialed his number but got voicemail. She surveyed the backyard quickly, stepped out on the patio, and called everyone in, despite much protest. A trail of water splashed all over the kitchen floor, through the living room, and up the stairway.

Brian held his arms out in a question.

"Call backup. Get dressed. Now," she said.

She texted Luke to call for backup as well, and he confirmed. "I have a truck that's been circling the block several times. Got the plates."

"Send a text to Hamish."

Her phone rang. "What's up?"

"Connor just confessed to being involved with this Nevada group. We need backup now, Hamish. I think they're coming to kill all of us."

Before Hamish could reply, a piercing zing flew through the living room window, as a high-powered round hit Connor perfectly on the temple and shattered his skull.

CHAPTER 17

BY THE TIME Hamish got to his house, the streets had been blocked off and no fewer than five fire engines and four ambulances, as well as a dozen SDPD cruisers, were scattered all over the neighborhood, littering the small hillside of quiet single-family homes. There was no place to park, so he took a driveway at a house he knew to be currently vacant and then ran the few yards to the blockade.

He'd been in contact with Luke by phone, who informed him the family was safe but explained there was one casualty. He and Brian remained inside the house in case there was a breech. Angie, Marie, and the three kids were upstairs, unharmed.

Hamish was glad he'd decided to leave Cora in the care of the new recruits. It was bad enough the other three were having to go through all this.

He knew Angie would get her Sig, and though they were seriously under-armed for an onslaught, if one were to occur, by the look of the equipment parked outside his house, he didn't think it was something to worry about.

His neighbor across the street, a member of the mayor's elite SWAT team, was wearing a tactical vest over his aloha shirt and shorts. He'd holstered his weapon, as had nearly half of the officers who showed up. Hamish walked over to him, just outside the blockade.

"Carl, never seen you so decked out," he said, chuckling.

"Thanks to this, I've got eight guests inside scared shitless and who will never come over to my place again for a barbeque."

Hamish laughed at him.

"Speaking of guests, what the hell were y'all doing here today on a fine fall Sunday afternoon?"

"I was moving boxes, but did you see the news last night about the raid near Imperial Beach?"

"Oh, the human smuggling thing? That was your caper?"

"Well, sort of. Whoever did this is connected. Do you know if they got the shooter?"

"I think he's in the truck. His driver got popped."

Hamish wanted to get a glimpse of the man's face, but he was sitting behind his cracked windshield, no doubt fully shackled. His buddy's blood was spattered all over the inside as he was hit from behind.

Carl sneered down at him. "You Navy guys have a wrong sense of priorities. It's real different. What the hell were you doing moving boxes and not defending your wife and kids?"

"It's a long story, but I had men here. They weren't unprotected."

"But the buzz on the radio says your guest got a brain cauterization all the way down to his Adam's apple. You're going to have to change the carpet."

"We have tile."

"Smart. Good forward thinking," he said, pointing to his temple. "Who was the dude?"

"A former Team Guy, a brother. He was about to become an informant, I understand from my wife."

"And she puts up with you, huh? Man, every one of my three wives would be all over my ass if I was helping somebody move while she was being shot at. You live under a lucky star. Yeah, you Navy dudes got some extraterrestrial help up there," he said, pointing to the sky, which was darkening.

"You know how it goes. Sailors navigate by the stars, Carl."

"So do I have to start hiring extra security now?"

"I don't think so. I think they're mopping up the gang. Next time, it will be someone else."

"So you work human trafficking now? That what

the Navy's into?"

"I'm former Navy. Now work as a Special Agent. We do a lot of stuff."

"Oh, a *Special* Agent. That's fine. Because on those videos I saw at the museum, they show you guys, when you were a Team Guy, sneaking onto the shore and then back out to sea, only leaving your flipper prints until the waves wash it away. Silent, stealth. Nobody knew you was there. Know what I mean?"

"Yup, I saw that video hundreds of times."

"Explain what about this operation is stealth…"

"Very funny. You forget, this was an attack. We didn't initiate it."

"Oh, that's the difference, then! Well, thanks for helping me out. Now, if you don't mind, I'm going to go back to my house, remove this bullet-proof vest, stow my piece, and try to calm down my guests. You have any idea how long before they can leave?"

"Carl, sport," Hamish said as he grabbed the man's shoulder and squeezed. Carl cowered, slightly, at the pressure. "Just as soon as they remove all these vehicles you see here. Then they can leave."

"Yeah, I knew all you Navy guys were smart. That's a smart answer too. Thanks, neighbor. I'll see you around. I'm never going to show up at your door without being previously announced."

He left, removing his vest as he did so, shaking his

head.

Hamish made a mental note that perhaps Carl drank whisky. At least he was going to research that.

Angie called. "Hey, I'm right outside. I can't get through."

"Thank God. Boy, I don't know how much of this I can take, Hamish. Tell me this is nearing a close."

"I'm guessing so, for now. You mind coming to the door and pointing me out so they'll let me in?"

"Sure."

He saw her step outside, scan the crowd, and point to him. The uniform outside shouted, "Sir, you may enter."

Hamish made his way in. Angie must have quickly gone back upstairs. He slowly walked past what was left of Connor. He'd really liked this house when they bought it. Now, with all this blood everywhere, he wasn't sure he wanted to ever come back to it. But he knew, he'd get over that soon. One odd thing he noticed was that Connor was still clutching a notebook in his right hand, a nice leather portfolio book with a gold logo on the outside, usually with a nice pen inside. He grabbed a sterile glove and removed the book. Connor had typed a full confession and given names and account numbers of several of the company's bank accounts, both in California, but also Nevada and the Bahamas.

He had some screenshots of texts he'd received on his cell from various officers of the company, tying them all together. Hamish picked up a large evidence bag from a box at his feet, placed the notebook inside, and squeezed the top to seal it.

Upstairs, Ian, Sasha and Andrew were talking in whispers. They were located in Sasha's room, listening to music.

"Hey, Dad. Glad you're home," Ian said as he got up and hugged him.

"Where's Mom?"

"Your bedroom. She's got a headache."

In Cora's bedroom lay the sleeping form of Marie. She clutched a tissue in one hand. Hamish had to admit he did feel sorry for her. It was going to be a long road ahead of her.

He took the five or six steps down the hallway, trying not to rattle the windows. Angie was spread-eagle on the bed, fast asleep, which must have happened immediately upon lying down, still clutching her Sig in her right hand.

She was his woman, in every way possible. She'd sacrifice the same as Hamish would to keep her family safe. She was his fearless partner in everything important to life itself.

IN THE ENSUING days, the task force, under Harper's

leadership, picked up over a hundred employees and contractors implicated in the criminal enterprise, including good old Bernie Isaacson, the member of Senator Nolan's staff.

Fredo was cleared of charges for the midnight hit-and-run, the investigators citing the damage to his truck and the pursuit in rescuing a hostage. They were found not to have initiated an attack, defending themselves and the minor child from harm in the process.

Admiral Patterson personally approved a requisition for a new truck for Fredo's family, as a bonus for a job well done. Fredo got to work right away installing his metal storage beneath the driver's seat to secure his weapons. His big objection was that the truck came in white, not red.

But barely a week later, word got to President Collier that the caravans had returned, following the same footprint. Another cartel had taken over the territory after a minor shootout in Mexico, leaving a dozen cartel junior members dead.

Sasha recorded over twenty hours of testimony, and because she was a minor, they could admit these into evidence without her having to appear in person. She was going to write a paper about the ordeal and turn it in for an English project.

Cora's team went on after their successful Sunday

matches to make a Junior National Team. There was going to be travel, and perhaps some international as well, but Hamish and Angie agreed she could go only if one of them accompanied her.

Senator Nolan acted surprised when he was seen on TV being told one of his staffers had been arrested. The president himself told Hamish he had special plans for the man and not to ask too many questions.

Hamish asked for, and was given permission for, a long vacation. He had something in mind.

Harper said he would miss him and please not to get injured, which he always said.

A series of investigative journalists were put on the story, and the public was told about the organization, with a thin thread connecting to Senator Nolan's office.

The buses were confiscated by Customs & Border Patrol, to be painted and used for their work transporting migrants all over the country.

The parish in Phoenix erected a bust of Father Flaherty in a small rose garden off the chapel. He was told weeks later that it was the new priest's favorite place to pray.

The renovations were being done to the house and would take approximately two months. In addition to a tear-out of the entry and living room spaces, a sophisticated security system was installed. Hamish would later have it customized further.

With the two months' time off, they pulled the kids out of school and took a long vacation. It was sort of like camping, he promised them. Though Angie and Cora were hesitant, with it being their daughter's senior year, they decided to make family a priority. Plus, she could keep up using remote learning.

Hamish had always wanted to own a big fancy bus like his favorite country music stars. He'd looked at them for years at the trade shows. He found a low mileage and extremely clean ten-year-old 42' Class A, with heated floors, a washer/dryer, and even a fireplace. It checked out mechanically and came with a killer stereo, two TVs, and an internet pod. It had four slide-outs and easily would sleep eight.

But all they needed was room for six, unless they got a dog.

CHAPTER 18

T HE KIDS WERE ecstatic when Hamish took them to view the new bus. They fiddled with all the gadgets, exploring the closets and the huge bathroom, to which Ian asked, "Only one?"

"We'll learn how to share, Ian. And to strategically use restaurant bathrooms along the trip, okay? And we'll bring spray, trust me. Maybe a carton of it."

That did seem to satisfy him.

"Does it have a horn?"

He didn't tell them he'd switched out the former one that played "La Cucaracha" and replaced it with a truck horn, which gave a satisfying bone-chilling blast. "A loud one." He got a cheer for that decision.

He hoped his others would go over as well.

He demonstrated the proposed sleeping arrangement. He and Angie would, of course, have the rear master bedroom. The boys would be over the cab in a platform that could be raised or lowered by a switch and contained a spacious double bed.

"You don't get your own bedrooms."

The girls would share the sofa, which made into a queen. They'd get to lounge watching the fireplace at night. There was still plenty of room for using the kitchen, bath, and storage areas when they utilized all the slide-outs. They each had their own under-seat storage, and that was the limit to what they could take. Angie told them they could even pick out the clothes and games they wanted, no restrictions.

He showed them the heated floors and how the fireplace could be turned on with a switch.

He and Angie held each other as they watched the kids inspect everything. He was pleased it was a hit.

"When do we take off?" asked Cora.

"Tomorrow morning, if you're ready."

They'd been housed at a nearby motel, so they needed to make one trip to the old house, still under inspection, to pick up items they wanted to bring. They took one last dip into the pool while Angie washed one last load of clothes and laid them out for everyone.

Hamish brought his container of ninety-day supply of food for emergencies, an extensive medical kit, some firepower, and extra boxes of ammunition, all locked and not visible to the outside. At Harper's insistence, he had installed a security system and tracking device so the Team could follow their travels, but still give the family privacy.

The family was still considered a high value target, but they were not accepting a security detail, unless necessary.

"How did we pay for this?" Angie asked him.

"The admiral funded me a loan. I'll be taking it out of my salary over the next ten years. I'm thinking we won't have it that long. When the kids are out of the house, we might get a fancier one, maybe brand new, so you and I can tour in style."

She was lukewarm about the idea.

"As long as it's with you. If you know how to oper- ate it, Hamish. That's a nice thought, but we have colleges to pay for, then maybe a wedding or two?"

"I won't do anything again unless I consult you. If we take this out, and we don't like it, we just sell it. A lot easier than selling a house."

"I don't want to sell my house, Hamish. I love my house."

"We won't. But let's give this a try. For two months, it will be an experiment in close proximity living. We can go when we want, where we want. We don't have to have a schedule. The kids can study while we're driving. Or we switch off, and you can drive, if you like."

"Not sure—"

"You'll love it. Just give it a try. It's really fun.

You're high above the traffic, great visibility. Just have to adjust to corners and bad drivers. Makes you feel like a fancy long-haul trucker!"

"Which I never wanted to be, but I'll give it a try. For you, I'll become a truck driver too."

"Look at it this way, less house cleaning. Less laundry."

"Better be."

"Got a built-in vacuum system." He winked at her.

"If it isn't for me, we can sell it?"

"My promise to you, my love. Honest Abe here."

She walked around, holding his hand as they inspected the compartments and studied the huge beast. He saw she was warming to the new adventure.

They headed north. The plan was to take the coastal route. None of them had ever done this before. The idea was to make it all the way up the Coast of California, through Oregon, and wind up in Seattle. Then they'd head back midland for a quicker way home.

The road was twisty in places, but at every turn, the stunning beauty of the Pacific Ocean and the surrounding countryside were easier to study with their slow pace. The kids frequently told their dad there were ten cars behind him and for him to pull over, which he pretty much obeyed, if he could.

They learned the first night out that parking a forty-two foot bus could be problematic and was hairy driving through city traffic, switching highways, or looking for places to stop. Not all campsites had facilities for this size. Some limited it to forty feet, but at one of the stops, he purchased software that could be added to his GPS system that would show him the Class A approved places.

Most of them had large recreation halls and pools, even miniature golf courses, with various activities sponsored by the site. The kids made friends, got just as much swimming time as they had at home, and traveled well.

Places they liked the best, they stayed longer, like they did in the Monterey Basin, Carmel, and then near San Francisco at Half Moon Bay, where they attended a pumpkin festival. They crossed the Golden Gate on a cloudless and fogless day and could see the Channel Islands far out to sea, which rarely appeared this time of year.

They traveled up through Wine Country, stopped at the Redwoods for a week of hang gliding and ziplines through the old growth forest. They explored old lumber towns, Mendocino, and on to the border. Oregon's rocky coast was beautiful. They attended a rodeo then stopped at several craft fairs since it was nearing the Holidays.

They'd made it to Seattle and spent Christmas Eve

on an island outside of the city, watching the lights. Even had a light dusting of snow.

Hamish barbequed a huge prime rib on the outside grill they brought. Though it was cold, and they bundled in blankets, they ate the tender meal by the light of the bonfire he'd built. They had almost the whole campsite to themselves. The local ranger stopped by for a glass of whiskey and toasted them a safe journey home.

The kids were in bed, and the cleanup was done. Hamish stood next to Angie, holding hands, by the firelight, looking over at the lights of Seattle.

"You are my Christmas gift, sweetheart," he said as he kissed the top of her head.

"As you are mine. Always have been. Even when I'm mad at you."

"When have you been mad at me? Aren't you having a good time?"

"The best. I have to admit, I thought you were off your rocker at first when you bought this thing. And ten years old?"

"Oh, these things, if they're cared for, go hundreds of thousands of miles. As long as they keep making diesel. And the gas models, they're slugs."

"I wasn't talking about the speed or the gas, Hamish."

"I know. I was deflecting. I don't want to know if

and when you were or are angry at me. I don't need to know that. It's Christmas Eve. We have everything we've wanted. We've learned a lot this year. The kids got exposed to things most will never see, and I'm thankful for that. It could have ended poorly."

"Right about that."

"You know what this is?"

"I think I do," Angie answered.

"This is freedom. This is the taste of what freedom really is. To be able to do this with the ones you love. It isn't slaving at a desk job all your life and then doing it when you retire."

"You're right, Hamish."

"I've traveled all over the world, and this country is still my favorite. And I aim to try to keep her that way. What a gift."

She was silent for a few minutes. She knew what he was thinking.

"Paid for by some of the ones who didn't come home," she whispered.

It was a combination of sadness and pride, but his heart was filled with tremendous appreciation for the sacrifices of others over the years to help create this imperfect country he loved so much.

We'll get it right, one day. I trust and have hope, someday, we'll look back on this as the beginning of a better world. But only if the ones who do the protecting

have the courage to stand up and be counted.
I am that man. This is worth everything.

Did you enjoy Silver Rescue?

Stay tuned, for Hamish and Angie's story will continue,
but when is a mystery, even to the author.

ABOUT THE AUTHOR

NYT and USA/Today Bestselling Author Sharon Hamilton's SEAL Brotherhood series have earned her author rankings of #1 in Romantic Suspense, Military Romance and Contemporary Romance. Her other *Brotherhood* stand-alone series are: Bad Boys of SEAL Team 3, Band of Bachelors, True Blue SEALs, Nashville SEALs, Bone Frog Brotherhood, Sunset SEALs, Bone Frog Bachelor Series, SEAL Brotherhood Legacy Series and SEAL Brotherhood: Silver Team. She is a contributing author to the very popular Shadow SEALs multi-author series.

Her SEALs and former SEALs have invested in two wineries, a lavender farm and a brewery in Sonoma County, which have become part of the new stories. They also have expanded to include Veteran-benefit projects on the Florida Gulf Coast, as well as projects in Africa and the Maldives. One of the SEAL wives has even launched her own women's fiction series under the pen name of Annie Carr. But old characters, as well as children of these SEAL heroes keep returning to all the newer books.

Under the pen name S. Hamil, she has a new Dystopian/Sci-Fi/Fantasy Romance, Free to Love. Book 1 of this 5-book series has been released: Free As A Bird. The story arc is about a future alternative universe where Androids are feared because of their AI capabilities that outpace human intelligence, and yet the hero, an android, may become the savior of the world, both human and other.

Annie Carr, Sharon's Women's Fiction author pen name, has just released her first two books in 2023, I'll Always Love You, and Back to You, in Sunset Beach stories. She is planning this to become a multiple-book series.

A lifelong organic vegetable and flower gardener, Sharon and her husband lived for fifty years in the Wine Country of Northern California, where many of her stories take place. Recently, they have moved to the beautiful Gulf Coast of Florida, with stories of shipwrecks, the white sugar-sand beaches of Sunset, Treasure Island and Indian Rocks Beaches.

She loves hearing from fans through her website:
authorsharonhamilton.com

Find out more about Sharon, her upcoming releases, appearances and news when you sign up for Sharon's newsletter.

Facebook:
facebook.com/SharonHamiltonAuthor

Twitter:
twitter.com/sharonlhamilton

Pinterest:
pinterest.com/AuthorSharonH

Amazon:

amazon.com/Sharon-Hamilton/e/B004FQQMAC

BookBub:

bookbub.com/authors/sharon-hamilton

Youtube:

youtube.com/channel/UCDInkxXFpXp_4Vnq08ZxM
BQ

Soundcloud:

soundcloud.com/sharon-hamilton-1

Sharon Hamilton's Rockin' Romance Readers:

facebook.com/groups/sealteamromance

Sharon Hamilton's Goodreads Group:

goodreads.com/group/show/199125-sharon-hamilton-
readers-group

Visit Sharon's Online Store:

sharon-hamilton-author.myshopify.com

Life is one fool thing after another.

Love is two fool things after each other.

REVIEWS

PRAISE FOR THE
SEAL BROTHERHOOD SERIES

"Fans of Navy SEAL romance, I found a new author to feed your addiction. Finely written and loaded delicious with moments, Sharon Hamilton's storytelling satisfies like a thick bar of chocolate." —Marliss Melton, bestselling author of the *Team Twelve* Navy SEALs series

"Sharon Hamilton does an EXCELLENT job of fitting all the characters into a brotherhood of SEALS that may not be real but sure makes you feel that you have entered the circle and security of their world. The stories intertwine with each book before...and each book after and THAT is what makes Sharon Hamilton's SEAL Brotherhood Series so very interesting. You won't want to put down ANY of her books and they will keep you reading into the night when you should be sleeping. Start with this book...and you will not want to stop until you've read the whole series and then...you will be waiting for Sharon to write the next one." (5 Star Review)

"Kyle and Christy explode all over the pages in this first book, *[Accidental SEAL]*, in a whole new series of SEALs. If the twist and turns don't get your heart jumping, then maybe the suspense will. This is a must read for those that are looking for love and adventure with a little sloppy love thrown in for good measure." (5 Star Review)

PRAISE FOR THE
BAD BOYS OF SEAL TEAM 3 SERIES

"I love reading this series! Once you start these books, you can hardly put them down. The mix of romance and suspense keeps you turning the pages one right after another! Can't wait until the next book!" (5 Star Review)

"I love all of Sharon's Seal books, but *[SEAL's Code]* may just be her best to date. Danny and Luci's journey is filled with a wonderful insight into the Native American life. It is a love story that will fill you with warmth and contentment. You will enjoy Danny's journey to become a SEAL and his reasons for it. Good job Sharon!" (5 Star Review)

PRAISE FOR THE
BAND OF BACHELORS SERIES

"*[Lucas]* was the first book in the Band of Bachelors series and it was a phenomenal start. I loved how we got to see the other SEALs we all love and we got a look at Lucas and Marcy. They had an instant attraction, and their love was very intense. This book had it all, suspense, steamy romance, humor, everything you want in a riveting, outstanding read. I can't wait to read the next book in this series." (5 Star Review)

PRAISE FOR THE
TRUE BLUE SEALS SERIES

"Keep the tissues box nearby as you read *True Blue SEALs: Zak* by Sharon Hamilton. I imagine more than I wish to that the circumstances surrounding Zak and Amy are all too real for returning military personnel and their families. Ms. Hamilton has put us right in the middle of struggles and successes that these two high school sweethearts endure. I have read several of Sharon Hamilton's military romances but will say this is the most emotionally intense of the ones that I have read. This is a well-written, realistic story with authentic characters that will have you rooting for them and proud of those who serve to keep us safe. This is an author who writes amazing stories that you love and cry with the characters. Fans of Jessica Scott and Marliss Melton will want to add Sharon Hamilton to their list of realistic military romance writers." (5 Star Review)

"Well to say the least I was thoroughly surprised. I have read many Vampire books, from Ann Rice to Kym Grosso and a few other Authors, so yes I do like Vampires, not the super scary ones from the old days, but the new ones are far more interesting, far more human than one can remember. I found Honeymoon Bite a totally engrossing book, I was not able to put it down, page after page I found delight, love, under-standing, well that is until the bad bad Vamp started being really bad. But seeing someone love another person so much that they would do anything to protect them, well that had me going, then well there was more and for a while I thought it was the end of a beautiful love story that spanned not only time but, spanned Italy and California. Won't divulge how it ended, but I did shed a few tears after screaming but Sharon Hamil-ton did not let me down, she took me on amazing trip that I loved, look forward to reading another Vampire book of hers."

"An excellent paranormal romance that was exciting, romantic, entertaining and very satisfying to read. It had me anticipating what would happen next many times over, so much so I could not put it down and even finished it up in a day. The vampires in this book were different from your average vampire, but I enjoy different variations and changes to the same old stuff. It made for a more unpredictable read and more adventurous to explore! Vampire lovers, any paranormal readers and even those who love the romance genre will enjoy Honeymoon Bite."

"This is the first non-Seal book of this author's I have read and I loved it. There is a cast-like hierarchy in this vampire community with humans at the very bottom and Golden vampires at the top. Lionel is a dark vampire who are servants of the Goldens. Phoebe is a Golden who has not decided if she will remain human or accept the turning to become a vampire. Either way she and Lionel can never be together since it is forbidden.

I enjoyed this story and I am looking forward to the next installment."

"A hauntingly romantic read. Old love lost and new love found. Family, heart, intrigue and vampires. Grabbed my attention and couldn't put down. Would definitely recommend."

"Dear FATHER IN HEAVEN,

If I may respectfully say so sometimes you are a strange God. Though you love all mankind,

It seems you have special predilections too.

You seem to love those men who can stand up alone who face impossible odds, who challenge every bully and every tyrant ~

Those men who know the heat and loneliness of Calvary. Possibly you cherish men of this stamp because you recognize the mark of your only son in them.

Since this unique group of men known as the SEALs know Calvary and suffering, teach them now the mystery of the resurrection ~ that they are indestructible, that they will live forever because of their deep faith in you.

And when they do come to heaven, may I respectfully warn you, Dear Father, they also know how to celebrate. So please be ready for them when they insert under your pearly gates.

Bless them, their devoted Families and their Country on this glorious occasion.

We ask this through the merits of your Son, Christ Jesus the Lord, Amen."

By Reverend E.J. McMalhon S.J. LCDR, CHC, USN
Awards Ceremony SEAL Team One
1975 At NAB, Coronado